PROPOSAL
AT THE
WINTER BALL

PROPOSAL AT THE WINTER BALL

BY

JESSICA GILMORE

MILLS & BOON

First published in Great Britain 2015
By Mills & Boon, an imprint of HarperCollins *Publishers*
1 London Bridge Street, London, SE1 9GF

Large Print edition 2016

© 2015 Jessica Gilmore

ISBN: 978-0-263-26181-3

Our policy is to use papers that are natural, renewable
and recyclable products and made from wood grown
in sustainable forests. The logging and manufacturing
processes conform to the legal environmental regulations
of the country of origin.

Printed and bound in Great Britain
by CPI Antony Rowe, Chippenham, Wiltshire

For Charlotte and Flo

Charlotte for so selflessly allowing me to pillage her commuting woes and for being such a brilliant sounding board, co-plotter, and very patient (and talented) editor.

Flo for making 'The Call' that changed everything, for guiding me so patiently through the whole publishing process, and for being a fab co-presenter extraordinaire and late-night wine-drinking companion.

Thank you both x

CHAPTER ONE

'A GLASS OF white wine and make it a large one.' Flora sank onto the low leather seat and slumped forward, banging her forehead against the distressed oak table a couple of times. She sat back up and slouched back in her chair. 'Please,' she added, catching a quizzical gleam in Alex's eyes.

'Bad day?' He held up a hand and just like that the waiter glided effortlessly through the crowds of office-Christmas-party escapees and Friday-night drinkers towards their table, tucked away in the corner as far from the excited pre-Christmas hubbub as they could manage. Flora could have waved in the waiter's general direction for an hour and he would have ignored her the whole time but Alex had the knack of procuring service with just a lift of a brow; taxis, waiters, upgrades on flights. It was most unfair.

What was it about Alex that made people—

especially women—look twice? His messy curls were more russet than brown, his eyes undecided between green and grey and freckles liberally splattered his slightly crooked nose. And yet the parts added up to a whole that went a long way beyond plain attractive.

But then Alex *was* charmed—while Flora's fairy godmother must have been down with the flu on the day her gifts were handed out. Flora waited not too patiently, ready to finish her tale of woe, while Alex ordered their drinks. A humiliation shared was a humiliation halved, right?

Finally the waiter turned away and she could launch back in. 'Bad day I could cope with but it's been a bad *wee*k. I think I'm actually cursed. Monday was the office manager's birthday and she brought in doughnuts. I bit into mine and splat. Raspberry jam right down the front of my blouse. Of course it was my nicest white silk,' she added bitterly.

'Poor Flora.' His mouth tilted with amusement and she glared at him. He was still in his work suit and yet looked completely fresh. Yep, unfairly charmed in ways that were completely wasted on a male. Flora's seasonally green wool dress was stain free today but she still had that slightly sticky, crumpled, straight-from-work feel and was pretty sure it showed...

'And then yesterday I left work with my skirt tucked into my knickers. No, don't laugh.' She reached across the table and prodded him, his chest firm under her fingers. 'I didn't realise for at least five minutes and...' this was the worst part; her voice sank in shame '...I wasn't even wearing nice knickers. Thank goodness for fifteen-denier tights.'

Alex visibly struggled to keep a straight face. 'Maybe nobody noticed. It's winter, surely you had a coat on?'

'I was wearing a jacket. A *short* jacket. And judging by the sniggering the whole of Holborn noticed. But even that was better...' Flora stopped short and buried her face in her hands, shame washing over her as she mentally relived the horror of just an hour ago.

'Better than?' Alex leaned back as the waiter

returned carrying a silver circular tray, smiling his thanks as the man put a pint in front of him and a large glass of wine in front of Flora. She picked up the glass, gratefully taking a much-needed gulp, the cold tartness a welcome relief.

'Better than tonight. I didn't mean to...' The old phrase tripped off her tongue. Flora's mother always said that they would be her last words, carved onto her grave.

Here lies Flora Prosperine Buckingham.
She didn't mean to.

'I was just so relieved to see a seat I all out ran for it only I threw myself in a little too vigorously, misjudged and I ended up...I ended up sitting on a strange man's knee.'

She glared at Alex as he choked on his pint. 'It's not funny! The whole carriage just stared at me and the man said...' She stumbled over the words, her cheeks heating at the memory. 'He said, "Make yourself comfortable, pet. I like a girl with plenty to grab hold of."'

She took another gulp, ignoring the guffaws

of laughter opposite. The words had stung more than she cared to admit. So she was tall with hips and a bosom that her mother called generous and her kinder friends described as curvy? In the nineteen fifties she would have been bang on trend but right now in the twenty-first century she just felt that bit too tall, that bit too wide, that bit too conspicuous.

Of course, sitting on a strange man's lap in a crowded Tube carriage hadn't helped her blend in. There had probably been people from her office in that very carriage on that very train, witnesses to her humiliation. Thank goodness her contract ended next week, although the thought of even one week of whispers and sniggers was bad enough; if only she could get a convenient dose of flu and call in sick. A week of rest, recuperation and isolation was exactly what she needed.

Though sick days meant no pay. Flora sighed. It was no fun temping.

Alex finally stopped laughing. 'That was very friendly of you. So you've made a new friend?'

'No!' She shuddered, still feeling an itch in the exact spots where the large hands had clasped her. 'The worst thing was I just had to sit there and pretend nothing had happened. No, not on his lap, idiot! On the seat next to him. I'm surprised I didn't spontaneously combust with mortification.'

How she would ever get back onto that Tube, onto that line, even onto the entire underground network again she had no idea. Maybe she could walk to work? It would only take a couple of hours—each way.

'Will you go back there after Christmas?' It was as if he had read her mind. Alex was far too good at that.

Flora shook her head. 'No, I was covering unexpected sick leave and she should be back after the holidays. Luckily January is always a good time for temps. All those people who decide to *carpe diem* on New Year's Eve or do something outrageous at the Christmas party.'

'Come on, Flora, is that your grand plan? Another year temping? Isn't it time you *carpe diem* yourself? Look, it's been two years since you were made redundant. I know it stung but shouldn't you be back in the saddle by now?'

Flora put her glass firmly on the table, blinking back the sudden and very unwanted tears. 'It's not that easy to find design work and at least this way I'm paying the bills. And no...' she put up her hand as he opened his mouth '...I am not moving in with you and I am not moving back home. I don't need charity. I can do this on my own.'

Besides, it wasn't as if she wasn't trying. Since she had been made redundant from her job at a large but struggling pub chain she had sent out her portfolio to dozens of designers, retail head offices and agencies. She had also looked for freelance work, all too aware how hard it was to land an in-house position.

Most hadn't even bothered to reply.

Alex regarded her levelly. 'I'm not planning on offering you charity. I'm actually planning to offer you a job.'

Again. Flora swallowed, a lump roughly the

size of the *Titanic* lodging itself in her throat. Just great. It wasn't that she envied Alex his incredible success; she didn't spend *too* much time comparing the in-demand, hotshot team of architects he headed up with her own continuing search for work. She tried not to dwell on the contrast between his gorgeous Primrose Hill Georgian terrace, bought and renovated to his exact design, and her rented room a little further out in the far ends of North London.

But she wished he wouldn't try and help her. She didn't need his pity. She needed him to believe in her.

'Look,' she said, trying to stop her voice from wobbling. 'I do appreciate you offering me work, just like I appreciate Mum needing a runner or Dad an assistant every time I'm between contracts. But if I learned anything from the three years I was with Village Inns it's that mingling the personal and the professional only leads to disaster.'

It *could* have been a coincidence that she was made redundant shortly after breaking up with the owner's son and heir apparent but she doubted it.

And yes, right now life was a struggle. And it was more than tempting to give in and accept the helping hands her family and best friend kept holding out to her. But if she did then she would just confirm their belief that she couldn't manage on her own.

At least a series of humiliating, weird or dull temp jobs kept her focused on getting out and getting on.

'I'm not offering you a role out of pity. I actually really need you. I need your help.' His mouth quirked into a half-smile.

Flora gaped at him. Had she heard right? The cheesy blend of Christmas tunes was already pretty loud and amplified even more by the group at the bar who were singing along a little too enthusiastically. 'You *need* me?'

That potentially changed everything.

'You know the hotel I designed in Austria?'

Did she know about the high-profile, high-concept boutique hotel Alex had designed for the über-successful, über-exclusive Lusso Group? 'You might have mentioned it once or twice.'

'I've been offered an exclusive contract to design their next three. They pick stunning natural locations, like everything to be as eco-friendly and locally sourced as possible and each resort has an entirely unique look and vibe. It's a fantastic project to work on. Only the designer I used for Austria has just accepted a job with a rival hotel brand and can't continue working with me.'

This was a lot bigger than the small jobs he had been pushing her way for the last two years. It was too big to be a pity offering; his own reputation was at stake as well. Hope mingled with pride and for the first time in a long, long time Flora felt a smidgen of optimism for her future.

Only to be instantly deflated by Alex's next words. 'I'm flying out tomorrow for the launch of the Austrian hotel and while I'm there I plan to present my initial concepts for the Bali hotel complete with the interiors and overall look. I thought Lola had at least made a start on it but when I called her today to ask her to fax her scheme over she told me cool as anything that, not only hadn't she started, but thanks to her new job she wasn't intending to.' He blew out a long breath, frustration clear on his face. 'This job better work out for her because there's no way I'll be recommending her again, no matter how insanely gifted she is.'

Ouch, ouch and ouch again. Flora's fingers tightened on her glass stem. So it wasn't her talent he was after, it was her availability?

But maybe it was time to swallow her pride. A job like this would propel her into the next league. She leaned forward, fixing an interested smile onto her face. 'So what do you want me to do? Study your plans and email my ideas over?' Her tiny box room of a bedroom, already crammed with material, her sewing machine and easel, wasn't the most inspiring surroundings but she could manage. Or she could travel back to her parents a week early and work from there—at least she would be warm and fed if not guaranteed any peace and quiet or, indeed, any privacy.

'Email? Oh, no, I need you to come to Austria with me. That way you'll get a real feel for their taste.' He fixed her with a firm gaze. 'You need to follow the brief, Flora. There's no room for your whimsy.'

Her whimsy? Just because her private designs were a little fantastical didn't mean she carried her taste into her professional work. She knew the difference between indulging her creativity in her personal work and meeting a client's brand expectations, no matter how dull they might seem. She narrowed her eyes at him. 'Of course, I *am* a professional.'

Alex held her gaze for a long second before nodding. 'Good. I'll talk you through my plans on the flight to Innsbruck'

The reality of his words hit her. A trip abroad. She hadn't been on a plane since her redundancy. 'Tomorrow? But I have another week of my temp job to go.'

'Can't you get out of it?'

'Well, yes. Although my agency won't be best pleased.'

'It's a temping agency. I'm sure they will be able to replace you.'

'Yes. Of course.' A fizz of excitement began to bubble through her. No more Tube trains and oppressive offices. No, she would be spending the next week in a gorgeous hotel. No more spreadsheets or audio typing or trying to put salespeople off, she would be flexing her creative muscles instead.

'It's a shame it isn't Bali. I could do with some winter sun.' Flora shivered despite the almost oppressive heat in the overcrowded wine bar. Her last holiday had been a tent in the Cornish countryside. It had all sounded idyllic on the website, which had deliriously described the golden beaches and beautiful scenery. The reality had been freak storms and torrential rain. She didn't think she'd been truly warm since.

Alex set down his pint. 'This isn't a holiday, Flora.'

'I know.' She leaned forward and grabbed his

hand. 'I was teasing you. I'd go to the Antarctic for a chance like this. What do I need to do?'

His fingers curled around hers, warm and strong, and Flora's heart gave the all too familiar and all too painful thump at his touch. 'Be ready tomorrow morning, early. Pack for snow and some glamorous events, you know the kind of thing.'

No, she didn't. Not recently but there was no way she was going to tell him that. 'Warm yet dressy. Got it.' A thought struck her as the group by the bar began to roar the chorus of yet another overplayed Christmas classic. 'When are we due back? Mum and Dad are expecting both of us home on Christmas Eve. They'd be gutted if you don't turn up. Horatio is on duty at the hospital so it'll just be Minerva, her perfect spouse and her perfect twins.'

She could hear the bitter note in her voice, feel it coat her tongue and took another sip to wash it down. What she meant was she couldn't cope with Minerva and her Stepford family without Alex.

'No Horry?' Alex raised his eyebrow. 'That's a shame. I do like watching your mum trying to fix him up with the local eligibles. He's so beautifully oblivious.'

'I think it's a defence mechanism.' Flora eyed Alex speculatively. 'Anyway, you should be glad he never takes the bait. If Mum wasn't worrying about her permanent bachelor son she might turn her matchmaking skills onto you.'

'You're her youngest child,' he countered sweetly. 'I wouldn't worry about me, Flora. It'll be you she'll be launching forth next.'

'Don't be ridiculous.' But she wasn't as sure as she sounded. Now thirty was just a year away there had been ominous rumbles about settling down along with the usual thinly veiled hints about getting a proper job, buying her own house and why couldn't she be more like her elder siblings? 'You're one of the family. Better. The Golden Boy. You know they think you can do no wrong.'

Alex had spent every single Christmas with the Buckinghams after the year his father and new stepmother had chosen to spend the festive season in St Bart's leaving eleven-year-old Alex at home in the housekeeper's charge. The next Christmas Flora and her family had taken it for granted he would join them, a stocking with his name on the chimney breast, a place set at the table.

Five years later he had packed his bags and left his father's house for good, taking up permanent residence in the attic bedroom next to Flora's own. He'd never told her just what had led up to his bitter estrangement from his father and Flora had never pried.

Turned out there were places even best friends didn't dare go.

'Don't worry, we'll be back for Christmas. There's no way I'm missing out on your father's Christmas dinner. He's promising goose this year. I watched him prepare it on a video on the Internet. Nothing is keeping me away.'

'That's all right, then.' She took a deep breath of relief. One day surely even Alex would manage more than six months with one of his identikit, well-bred girlfriends and would have to spend the holiday season with *her* family, not the Buckinghams. Each year they managed to hold onto him was a bonus.

She stared at her empty glass regretfully. 'If I need to pack, find my passport and be ready before the crack of dawn I'd better get going. What time shall I meet you?'

'Oh, no.' Alex pushed his chair back and stood up, extending a hand to Flora to help her out of her seat. 'I'm not risking your timekeeping, Flora Buckingham. I'll send a car for you. Five a.m. sharp. Be ready.'

Alex looked down at his tablet and sighed. So much for briefing Flora on the flight—although to be fair he should have known better. It was a gift he envied in her. No matter where they were, what the time was, she would fall asleep at the first sign of motion. She'd slumbered as the taxi took them through the dark, wintry predawn streets of London to the airport, waking long enough to consume an enthusiastic breakfast once they had passed through passport control, only to fall back asleep the second the plane began to taxi down the runway.

And now she was snoozing once again. She would definitely give Sleeping Beauty a run for her money. He elbowed her. 'Flora, wake up. I want you to take a look at this.'

'Mmm?' She stretched. 'I wasn't asleep, just dozing. Oh! Look at that.' She gazed, awestruck, out of the car windows at the snow-covered mountains, surrounding them in every direction. 'It's just like a Christmas card.'

'What do you think—is it as pretty as you imagined?'

She turned to him, mouth open in indignation, and he stifled a smile. She was far too easy to wind up. 'Pretty? It's so much more than mere prettiness. And look, there are actual chalets. Everywhere!'

'Well observed, Sherlock.'

She didn't react to his sardonic tone. 'I didn't realise Austrian people actually lived in them. I thought it was like thatched cottages. You know, people assume England is all half-timber and cottage gardens but in reality you're far more likely to live in some identikit house on a suburban estate. Oh, I wish I lived in a chalet. They are utterly beautiful.'

'I hope you feel the same way about the hotel.' It was the moment of truth. She had a keen eye, could always see straight through to the heart of his ideas. Would she appreciate the stark simplicity of the hotel, or think it too modern, anachronistic in this natural paradise?

'I always love your designs but this one sounds even more exciting than usual; I have to admit I am really looking forward to seeing it in all its finished glory.'

The car had been steadily taking them along the busy roads that led towards the Tyrolean capital, Innsbruck, but now it veered away to follow a smaller road that wound ahead, climbing into the footholds of the Alps. The snow lay inches upon inches deep on the sides of the roads.

'Just look at it, look at the light.' Flora's fingers flexed. 'Oh, why didn't I pack my sketchbook? Not that I could really capture it, not the way the sun plays on the snow. Not that light— it's like a kaleidoscope.'

A knot unravelled in the pit of Alex's stomach. She saw what he saw. The interchange between light and the snow. She would get the hotel.

'I have never seen so much snow in my life, not if I took every winter and added them together.' Yep, she was fully awake now, her dark eyes huge as she stared out at the mountains. 'How come England grinds to a halt at just the hint of snow and yet everything here is running normally despite tonnes of the stuff?'

'Because this stuff is what keeps the local economy ticking over. You can't market yourself as a winter wonderland without the cold white stuff.'

'It's like Narnia.' Flora leaned back and stared with enraptured eyes as the car took them higher and higher. On one side the mountains soared high above them, on the other the town was spread out like a child's toy village, the river cutting through the middle like an icily silver scarf. 'How much further? I thought the hotel was in Innsbruck itself.'

'No, it's above the town, close to the ski lifts. The guests are transported in and out at will so they get the best of both worlds. That's the idea anyway, nothing too much effort for them.'

'They are paying enough for it,' Flora pointed out. 'I cannot believe I get to stay somewhere this luxurious. Even the staff quarters are probably one up on a tent in the rain.'

'You're not in the staff quarters. Could you really see Lola in anywhere but a suite? You're doing her job, you get her room. Tomorrow is the soft opening so nobody who stays at the hotel this week is an actual paying guest. We'll be helping to wow travel journalists, bloggers and some influential winter sports enthusiasts.'

He paused, searching for the right words. He knew how awkward she felt in crowds and amongst strangers. 'Flora, it's crucial that they all leave at the end of the week completely bowled over. And it's equally crucial that I leave with fully approved designs. You can manage, can't you? I can't emphasise enough what a big deal this week is. For me, for my firm as well as for Lusso Hotels.'

'Really? How good of you to warn me. I might have put my foot in it otherwise.'

Warning bells tolled through Alex's mind. She sounded frostier than the branches on the trees outside. It was the same tone she'd used the day he'd told her that one day she would grow out of boy bands, the tone she'd used the day he had told her that her first boyfriend wasn't good enough. The same tone she'd used the never to be forgotten day she'd chopped her hair into a pixie cut and he had agreed that, yes, she did look more like a marine than like Audrey Hepburn.

'I only meant…'

'I know what you mean: be professional, don't mess this up. Well, I won't. I need this too, Alex. I might not have founded a "Top Ten Up and Coming Business" while in my twenties, I might not be the bright young thing in my profession. Not yet. I have a lot to prove and this is my big chance. So don't worry about me. I've got this covered.'

Alex opened his mouth to point out that she hid in the kitchen at every single party she attended and would rather face a den full of lions than make small talk but he shut it again. He needed to warn her just how much networking lay ahead of her but not now. He'd wait until she was a little mellower.

Luckily the car turned down a single-track road, cut into the side of the mountain, a dramatic drop on one side showcasing the valley spread out below. 'We're here,' he said instead with some relief. The car slid to a stop and Alex unbuckled his seat belt. 'This *is* Der Steinadler— The Golden Eagle. What do you think?'

She had been looking at him intently, forcing her point home, but at his words she turned and looked out of the window. Her mouth fell open. 'Holy cow. You did this? This is it?'

'Yep, what do you think?'

'I…' She didn't answer, clambering out of the car instead, muttering as her trainer-clad foot sank into the snow and pulling her quilted jacket more closely around her as the sharp chill of the wintry mountain air hit. She turned to him as he joined her. 'All that time spent playing with building blocks as a kid wasn't wasted, huh?'

The hotel was built on the narrow Alpine shelf and looked as if it were suspended above Innsbruck spread out in the valley below, the mountains opposite a living, breathing picture framed through the dramatic windows. Alex had eschewed the traditional chalet design; instead he had used the locally sourced golden wood as a frame for great sheets of glass. The hotel should have looked out of place, too industrial for the tranquil setting, and yet somehow it blended in, the trees and mountains reflecting back from the many panes of glass.

Every time he saw it, it was like being punched in the chest. He couldn't believe he had made his ambitious vision a reality. 'You like?'

Her cheeks were glowing and her large, full mouth curved into a smile. 'I love it. Alex, it's wonderful.'

Relief flooded through him. He wasn't sure why her opinion mattered so much. It wasn't just that she was his oldest friend. No, he trusted her taste. If she didn't get it then he wouldn't have communicated his vision properly. 'Come on, then. Let's go inside. I think you might combust when you see the swimming pool.'

CHAPTER TWO

'SHOW ME AROUND, ALEX! It's not every day a girl gets the architect providing the grand tour.'

'Don't you want to see your room and freshen up first?'

She shook her head. 'No, I'm quite fresh, thank you, and you can conclude the tour at my room.' Flora watched the bellboy pile her bags and coat onto his trolley and sighed happily. 'This is a lot better than lugging a tent over three fields—and then having to go back for the beds. Besides, you want me to get an idea of what the client wants? The best way is for me to take a detailed look around.'

Her first impression was of luxurious comfort rather than cold, chic elegance. The whole interior of the hotel was the same mix of glass and wood as the outside but softened with warm colours and plenty of plants, abstract prints and comfy-looking cushions and sofas to mellow the potentially stark effect.

Alex shrugged off his designer ski jacket, a coat that had probably cost more than Flora's entire suitcase of clothes, and gestured. 'Where do you want to start?'

'Bottom and work our way up?'

'Okay, then, get ready to combust. We're heading down to the pool.'

If Flora didn't actually burst into excitable flames when she saw the swimming pool it was a close-run thing. Housed a floor below the hotel entrance in a space carved out of the alpine shelf, the high-ceilinged pool was enclosed by a dramatic wall of glass. Swimming up to the edge of the pool must feel like swimming to the very edge of the mountain itself, she thought, staring out at the white peaks, as if you might plunge over the side, dive down to the valley below.

The lights were low and intimately flattering, padded sofas were dotted around in discreet corners, and whirlpools, saunas and steam rooms were hidden away behind glazed sliding doors.

Tables held jugs of iced water and inviting platters of fruit; thick fluffy towels were piled up on wooden shelves.

'Oh.' She pivoted, taking in every single detail. 'I just want to grab a magazine from that beautifully overstuffed bookshelf, pull on a robe and move into this room for ever. May I? Please?'

But Alex ignored her. 'Come on, next stop the lounge and then I'll take you to your room.'

By the time they reached her room Flora had scribbled down plenty of notes and photographed enough details to give her a good place to start. Obviously the designs she came up with for the Bali hotel would need to be unique, to marry with Alex's vision and the setting, but it was good for her to have an idea of the owner's tastes. She could see why Lola had used the palate she had; it was warming, sumptuous and complemented the natural materials prevalent throughout the building. The soft furnishings and décor were all shades of soft cream, gold, bronze and orange, whether it was the bronze and orange stripes on the cushions or the subtle champagne of the robes and the towels, the same colour in the crisp blouses and shirts worn by the staff.

It was clear that whatever look she designed for the Bali hotel would have to flow through every single detail, no matter how tiny.

'Okay.' Alex stopped at a cream door and gestured. 'This is you.'

Flora held her breath as she slid her keycard into the slot and turned the handle. Yes, she was here to work but there was no reason why she shouldn't enjoy it and after a few long years of penny-pinching and worrying it was rather splendid to be in such indulgent surroundings.

She stepped in and stopped, awestruck. 'Wow. Oh, Alex.'

At one end was the ubiquitous wall of glass and the ubiquitous stunning winter-wonderland view—not that it was getting old. Flora thought she could live here for ever and it would still be as breathtaking as the very first heart-stopping glimpse. The ceiling was high, arched and beamed, the walls a pale gold. The bed, a floating platform, was made up in white linen accented with a bronze silk throw and matching cushions.

Her suitcase had been placed on a low chest at the foot of the huge bed, the cheap, battered case more than a little incongruous in the spacious, luxurious suite. A reminder that this luxury was borrowed, that she had to earn her place here. Now she was here the jeans, jumpers and one good dress she had packed didn't seem enough. Not for the weather or for the hotel itself.

'You like it?' Alex stepped into the room, a smile playing on his lips as he watched her dart around, peering into every door.

'Like it? Do you realise that this walk-in wardrobe is bigger than my bedroom? In fact this suite is bigger than the house I live in—and I'm including the garden!'

She stopped by the glass screen that separated her bed from the small seating area and stared at the other screen, which stood between her bed and the bath, a huge tub affair perched on a dais right in the centre of the room.

'Thank goodness the toilet's in its proper place and not on show, otherwise this would feel more like an oddly luxurious prison cell than a hotel room!'

'It's looking good.' Alex took a few steps further in and turned slowly. 'I haven't seen most of the suites since they were decorated and the fixtures installed.' He stopped by the bath and ran one finger along the bronze trim. 'At least you'll be clean while you're staying here. It can be so difficult to drag oneself away from the bed to the bathroom, don't you find?'

Flora tested out the sofa, wincing as the rigidity of the cushions rejected her attempt to relax. It looked good but she wasn't sure she would want to actually sit on it for any length of time. 'Was the bath in the centre of the room your idea, Mr Fitzgerald? Have you been watching *Splash* again because I don't think there are many mermaids in the Austrian Alps.'

He grinned. 'Nope, not guilty, the fixtures are all Lola's vision. Apparently this particular suite is the epitome of romantic.'

'That's where I've been going wrong, all that old-fashioned bathing in private nonsense. Although it could be just a *leetle* awkward if I was sharing a room with a friend, not a romantic interest. Is this…erm…motif in all the rooms?'

'Not at all,' he assured her. 'In most of them the baths are tucked away respectably in the room for which they were intended. Okay. If you are ready, they are laying out *Kaffee und Kuchen* for us. I thought we could go and look through my design ideas in the lounge while we have a snack.'

'*Kaffee and Kuchen?* Coffee and cake?' Flora jumped to her feet. 'Never did words so gladden a girl's heart. I'm ready. Lead on, Macduff. Take me to cake.'

The coffee and cakes were laid out in the lounge, the social heart of the hotel, situated on the ground floor at the very front of the building to ensure it took full advantage of the stunning views. Once again Flora stood by the huge floor-to-ceiling windows and her stomach fell away at the terrifying illusion that there was nothing between her and the edge of the mountain.

Clusters of comfy bronze and red velvet sofas and chairs surrounded small tables, bookshelves full of books, games and magazines filled one wall and a huge wood-burning stove was suspended in the middle of the room. Somehow the lounge managed to feel cosy despite its vast size, easily capable of seating the sixty people the boutique hotel was designed to hold.

'Right.' Alex seated himself on one of the sofas and laid out his sketch pad in front of him. It would, she knew, be filled with exquisite pen-and-ink drawings. This was just the first phase, the visionary one. From here he would proceed to blueprints, to computer models, to hundreds of measurements and costings and attention to a million tiny little details that would transfer his vision from the page to reality.

But she knew this, the initial concept, was his favourite part. In many ways neither of them had changed that much from the children they had once been, designing their dream houses, palaces, castles, tree houses, igloos, ships in absorbed companionship.

But in other ways… She ran her eyes hungrily over him, allowing herself one long guilty look at the bent tousled head, at the long, lean body. In other ways they had both changed beyond recognition—not that Alex had noticed that.

No, in his eyes she was still the dirty-faced, scabby-kneed little girl he had met the first time he had run away from home. He'd only made it half a mile along the lane before bumping into Flora and together they'd built him a den to stay in. Planned for Flora to bring him bread and milk and a blanket.

He loved her, she knew that. And there weren't very many people who could claim that. Outside Flora's own family probably none.

He just wasn't *in* love with her. There had been a time, way back when, she had wondered. But her one attempt to move things up a level had ended messily.

Flora curled her fingers into fists, trying to block out the memory. Block out the way he had put his hands on her shoulders, not to pull her in closer but to push her away. Block out the look of utter horror in his eyes.

He had kissed a lot of girls that summer and subsequent springs, summers, autumns and winters. But not Flora; never Flora.

And here she was, all these years later, still hoping. Pathetic. One day she'd stop being in love with him. She just had to try a little harder, that was all.

Neither of them noticed the light outside fading, replaced by the gradual glow of the low, intimate hotel lighting. It wasn't until the huge Christmas tree dominating the far corner of the lounge sprang into brightly lit colour that Alex sat back, took off his work glasses and rubbed his eyes.

'So, what do you think?'

Flora chewed on her lip. 'I think I really need to take a trip out there to fully get your vision,' she said solemnly. 'At least three weeks, all-expenses-paid.'

'Play your cards right, convince Camilla Lusso that you can do this and you will do,' he pointed out. 'I told you that part of the brand promise is ensuring each hotel is both unique and part of its environment—and to leave as small a carbon footprint as possible. You'll need to source as much from local suppliers as possible.'

'Very worthy.' Flora pulled the pencil out of her hair and allowed the dark brown locks to fall onto her shoulders. 'Will the guests arrive in a canoe, paddled only by their own strokes with the help of a friendly wind?'

He bit back a grin. Trust Flora to see the big glaring hole in the whole eco-resort argument. 'Unlikely. But it's a start, don't knock it.'

'If I get to travel to Bali I promise not to give it as much as a second thought. Do you think they'll go for it? The glass-bottomed hotel?'

'I don't know. They've already decided to set the hotel in the rainforest—which is a pretty interesting decision. After all, most people expect a sea view in a place like Bali, so I really want to still have that water element. And although it would be nice to build out over the sea the local laws won't allow it—and the whole "surrounded by the sea" concept is a little "honeymoon in the Maldives" obviously.'

'Obviously.' Flora sounded wistful and he nudged her.

'Come on, work with me here. If I can't convince you I'm doomed. I actually think this might be even more breathtaking. Not just building over the lagoon but using glass floors to make the lagoon part of the hotel—the water as one of the design materials.'

'And I can bring that detail to bear inside. The lovely local dark woods and the natural blues and greens. Yes.' She nodded. 'I can work with that. Thanks, Alex.'

Alex pushed himself to his feet and walked over to the bar, a long piece of polished oak on the other side of the room. 'Glass of wine or a stein of Austrian beer?'

'I'm not sure what a stein is. A glass of white wine please.'

Alex ordered their drinks from the barmaid who was hovering discreetly at the far end.

He carried their drinks over and handed her the wine, taking a long appreciative gulp of his own cold beer, a heavy weight in the traditional stein glass. 'Cheers, or should I say *prost*?'

She raised her glass to his. 'Cheers. You were right. A job like this is just what I need.'

Alex paused. He knew it wasn't easy for her, younger sister to such high-achieving siblings, daughter of well-known experts in their fields. He knew her mother's well-intentioned comments on everything from Flora's hair to her clothes cut her to the quick. He knew how self-conscious she was, how she hated her conspicuous height, her even more conspicuous figure, her dramatically wide mouth and showy Snow White colouring. She really truly didn't know how stunning she was—when she wasn't hunching herself inside one of the sacklike dresses or tunics she habitually wore.

But she was twenty-nine now. It was time she believed in herself.

'You could have had work before,' he pointed out. 'How many times have I asked you to free-lance for me? You were just too proud to accept—or too afraid.'

Her mouth shut again, her lips compressed into a tight, hurt line. 'There's nothing wrong with wanting to stand on my own two feet.'

'No, there isn't.' He fought the urge to back-track; he'd always hated upsetting her in any way. 'But there's nothing wrong with accepting a helping hand either. Sometimes I think you're so determined to prove yourself you actually hold yourself back.'

Her eyes blazed. 'I can't win, can I? Once you accused me of not knowing my own mind, now you're telling me I'm too stubborn.'

'If you mean I told you not to apply to vet school then I stand by that. Just like I stand by telling you not to take that job at Village Inns. I still don't know why you did.'

Flora set her wine down on the table and glared at him. 'Why were you so set against it? No one lands the perfect job straight from college. It made sense to get some experience.'

'No, but your heart was never in that job, just like it wasn't in veterinary medicine. You applied for that to please your mum.'

Flora jumped to her feet and walked over to the window, staring out at the dark before turning to face him. 'So you were right that I wasn't vet material. Right that I couldn't hack it. So it took me a while to work things out. Excuse me for not being driven, focused on the goal like you, Mr Super Architect of the Year.'

He ignored the dig. So he was driven. Wasn't that the point? It was why they were here after all. 'Art school was far more you—but then you took the first safe job you could find even though designing those trendy pubs and twee restaurants drove you crazy. And when that didn't work out you went into lockdown mode. Took it personally, as if *you* had failed.'

'No, I didn't!' She paused, looked down at the floor. 'Well, maybe a little.'

'Look, Flora. You know the last thing I want

to do is hurt you. In any way.' It was truer than she knew. Alex didn't know where he would have ended up, what he would have been without Flora's friendship. It was why he had never been able to confide in her, not fully. He had never wanted to see the warmth in her eyes darken and chill. To be judged by her and found wanting.

God knew he judged himself enough for both of them.

'Thank goodness.' She looked at him directly then, her blue eyes shadowed. 'I'd hate to hear what you would say if you wanted to hurt me.'

'I just want you to follow your dreams. *Yours*, not your mother's or mine or trying to beat your sister at her own game. I want you to go for what you want. Do what makes you happy. Not hang back for fear it doesn't work out or in case you get knocked down again. Take each rejection as a challenge, get back up and try again. Harder each time. Here is your chance. Seize it.'

'I was trying to before my temporary boss and arrogant best friend decided to have a go at me.' But the anger had drained out of her voice. 'I'm not so good at the seizing, Alex. We didn't all get the Masters of the Universe education, you know.'

Alex had hated every single day at his elite boarding school. The only thing in its favour was that every day he had spent there was a day not at home. 'I dropped out of sixth form to slum it at college with you so I missed the Advanced World Domination course. But I tell you what I do know, Flora. We're all mostly faking it. Tell yourself you can do it, tell yourself you deserve it and make yourself go for it. That's the secret. Now, I don't know about you but those cakes seem like hours ago and I know the kitchen is hoping to do a last trial run on us before the guests arrive tomorrow. Let's go eat.'

'That was amazing. Although I don't feel I can ever eat again.' Flora patted her stomach happily and curled up on the velvet sofa.

'Not that cosy though, just the two of us in a room set for sixty.'

'Oh, I don't know.' It had felt a bit incongruous at first, the two of them waited on alone in a vast room, but a couple of glasses of the delicious wine had soon set her at her ease and when Alex suggested they went back into the lounge for one last look at the plans and a *digestif* her original plans for a bath and an early night were forgotten.

She had only drunk schnapps once before and it hadn't been pretty. But it was the national drink, after all; it would be rude not to sample it.

Alex was leaning back in his chair, his glass held loosely in his hand. Flora was usually so very careful about how she looked at him. If he ever caught her staring. If he ever guessed how she felt…

Alex was her oldest and best friend. His was the shoulder she cried on after break-ups and heartbreaks. He was her go-to person for advice. He knew all her vices and nearly all her secrets. But there were two things that lay between them. Two secrets; a chasm that could never be bridged.

He had never confided in her why he had left

home, and why he was so against any kind of reconciliation with his father.

And she had never told him that she loved him.

Not as a friend, as a confidant, but in every way it was possible for a woman to love a man. Sometimes Flora thought she had fallen for him that very first day, that skinny red-headed boy with a look of determination on his face—and desolation in the stormy eyes. The hair had long since darkened to a deep auburn, his body had filled out in all the right places, but he was still determined.

And he hid it well, but at heart he was still as alone as he had been then. Not one of his girlfriends had ever got through to him. Was that why she had never told him how she felt? He was right, she *was* afraid.

Afraid of not being good enough for him. Afraid he would turn away in disgust and horror, just as he had all those years ago. Afraid that this time she would lose him for ever.

Flora downed the schnapps in one satisfying gulp, choking a little as the pungent, sharp liquor hit the back of her throat. Hmm, not as bad as she'd thought. In fact, that warm feeling at the pit of her stomach was really quite pleasant. She refilled her glass.

She gazed into the amber depths as his words rolled round and round her mind. *'Get back up and try again. Tell yourself you deserve it.'* He was right. She never had. She took every rejection as a final blow whether it was work or her heart. It was easier not to put herself out there. Easier to lock herself away and hope.

Hope that somebody would see her Internet site and say, 'Hey, you amazing talent, come work for me!'

Hope that Alex would turn round, look into her eyes and realise, just like that, she was the only girl for him.

Hope that her parents would tell her that she made them proud.

She just sat back and let life pass her by. Hoping.

Flora raised her glass and downed the schnapps. It wasn't quite as fierce this time. Not as hot.

More…mellow. She had definitely underrated schnapps.

She reached out and closed her hand around the bottle, wondering why it took a few goes to clasp it properly, and pulled it towards her.

'Another one?' Alex's eyebrows rose. 'We had quite a lot of wine at dinner. Are you sure?'

'Yes, Dad.' She grinned at him. 'I like your hair like that.'

Alex touched his head, staring at her in confusion. 'My hair?'

Flora put her head to one side. 'It's all glowy with the Christmas lights behind you. Like a halo. Angel Alex.'

She didn't see him move but the next thing she knew he was by her side, one firm hand on hers, removing the bottle from her grasp.

'If you're talking about angels then you have definitely had enough. Come along.' He slid the bottle out of her reach and pulled at her hand, helping her rise to her feet. Flora swayed and caught his shoulder and he grimaced. 'Bed time for you. I forgot you and schnapps don't mix.'

'We mix just fine.' Flora regained her footing and stopped still, her hand still on his shoulder. She loved that Alex was taller than her. She looked up at him, his dearly familiar face so close to hers. The greeny-grey of his changeable eyes, the long lashes, the faded freckles on his nose, the curve of his cheekbones. The curve of his mouth. So close. Kissing distance. Her stomach clenched, the old exquisite pain. And yet all she had to do was stand on her tiptoes, just a little, and move in.

His words ran through her mind. *Try again. Harder each time.*

Maybe that was all she had to do. Try again. Maybe Alex was waiting for her to step forward, to make the move. Maybe it had always been within her power to change things but she had just never dared.

Maybe…

Before she knew it the words were tumbling out, words she had spent the last thirteen years keeping locked up deep, deep inside, more plaintive than demanding. 'Why didn't you kiss me back?'

'What?' His eyes widened in alarm and he took a step back. She moved with him, still holding on as if he were all that kept her anchored. He was lean, almost rangy, but there was a solidity when she touched him, the feel of a man who was fighting fit. 'What are you talking about?'

'All those years ago. Why did you push me away? Have you never wondered what would have happened if you hadn't?'

'It's never crossed my mind.' But his eyes shifted to her mouth as he spoke.

He's lying. Her throat dried as she realised what that meant.

He *had* thought about it. And that changed everything. Almost unconsciously she licked her lips; his throat tightened as he watched the tip of her tongue dip onto her top lip and, at the gesture, her heart began to beat faster.

Emboldened, Flora carried on, her voice low and persuasive. 'All those nights we stayed up talking till dawn. When we visited each other at uni we slept in the same bed, for goodness' sake. The tents we've shared... Have you never wondered, not even once? What it would be like? What *we'd* be like?'

'I…' His eyes were on hers, intent, a heat she had never seen before beginning to burn bright, melting her. 'Maybe once or twice.' His voice was hoarse. 'But we're not like that, Flora. We're more than that.'

Flora was dimly aware that there was something important in his words, something fundamental that she should understand, but she didn't want to stop, not now as the heat in his eyes intensified, his gaze locking on hers. If she pushed it now, he would follow. She knew it; she knew it as she knew him.

She also knew that whatever happened the consequences would be immense. There would be repercussions. Last time they had pretended it had never happened. It was unlikely that would happen again; their friendship would be altered for ever. Could she live with that?

Could she live without trying? Laugh it off as lack of sleep and too much schnapps? Now she had come so far…

No, not when he was looking at her like that. Heat and questions and desire mingling in his eyes, just as she had always dreamed. *I want you to go for what you want.* That was what he'd told her.

She wanted him.

'Kiss me, Alex,' she said softly. And before he could reply or pull away Flora stepped in, put her other hand on his shoulder and, raising herself on her tiptoes, she pressed her mouth to his.

CHAPTER THREE

HE SHOULD HAVE walked away. No, he *should* walk away, there was still time. Only there wasn't. Time was slowing, stopping, converging right here, right now on this exact spot, somewhere above Innsbruck. All that was left was this moment. The feel of her mouth against his, her hands, tentative on his shoulders. He shouldn't, he couldn't—and yet he was…

Because it was all he had dreamed it might be, those shameful, secret dreams. The crossing of boundaries, the touching the untouchable. Her touch was light, her kiss sweetly questioning and despite everything Alex desperately wanted to give her the answers she was seeking.

He stood stock-still for one long moment, trying to summon up the resolve to walk away, but the blood hummed through his veins, the noise drowning out the voice of caution; her sweet, vanilla scent was enfolding him and he was lost. Lost in her. Lost in the inevitable.

With that knowledge all thought of backing off, backing out disappeared. One hand slipped, as if of its volition, around the curve of her waist, pulling her in tightly against him, the other burying itself in the hair at the nape of her neck; a heavy, sweet smelling cloud. And Alex took control. He kissed her back, deepening, intensifying the kiss as the blood roared in his ears and all he could feel was the sweetness of her mouth, the softness of her body, pliant against his.

Her touch was no longer tentative, one arm tight around his neck. Holding his head as if she didn't dare let him go. The other was on the small of his back, working at the fabric of his shirt, branding him with the fevered heat of her touch.

If she touched his flesh he would be utterly undone.

Like the animal he was he could take her here and now. Not caring about the consequences, not caring that they weren't in a private space. That the staff could walk in any minute. That once again there would be no going back.

That once again he could take things too far. And once again he could lose everything.

He had learned nothing.

Alex wrenched his mouth away; the taste of her lingered, intoxicatingly tempting on his tongue. But he had to sober up. 'Flora.' His breath was ragged as he stared into her confused dark eyes. 'I...'

'Am I interrupting something?' Both Alex and Flora jumped slightly as the rich, Italian tones, tinged with a hint of mockery, floated across the hotel lounge. Alex didn't need to look around to know who he would see—the owner of this hotel and the woman who had employed him to design three more, Camilla Lusso.

'*Buongiorno*, Camilla.' He took a deep, shuddering breath, willing his overheated body to cool, his spinning brain to slow. 'I wasn't expecting to see you until tomorrow.' He turned, fixing a cool, professional smile on his face as he greeted his biggest and most influential client.

'That's rather clear.' Still that hint of mockery in her voice, her eyes assessing and cool as she looked at Flora, clearly not missing a single detail as she took in the mussed hair, the swollen lips, the wrinkles in the baggy dress.

Camilla Lusso could have been any age between thirty-five and fifty-five although Alex suspected she was at the top end of the age range, but her expensively styled hair, subtle make-up and chic wardrobe made her seem timeless. A glossy, confident and successful woman. A professional woman who demanded top-class professionalism from everyone who worked with and for her.

Flora was supposed to be impressing her, not being found drunkenly making out with the architect.

Why now? Why tonight after all these years? He could blame the schnapps, he could blame the mountains framed through the windows, the warmth of the fire burning in the stove. It was a scene out of *Seduction 101*. But the only person he could really blame was himself. He should have backed off, backed away, laughed off the conversation—not been struck dumb with the thought of an alternate world. A world in which he might have been worthy of the adoration and desire shining out of Flora's dark eyes.

He had to fix this. Camilla's eyes had narrowed as she assessed Flora. If she found her wanting in any way then Alex knew she'd turn her away, no matter how good her work.

'I owe you an apology, Camilla. When I recommended Flora to you I wanted you to appreciate her for her own talent and so...' He paused, searching for the right words, the right way to make this all right. There was only one way. To make the whole embarrassing scene seem perfectly normal.

'I didn't tell you that we're dating. I'm sorry, I should have mentioned it but we agreed to be discreet this week, to put our relationship on the back burner.' He allowed himself a wry smile. 'Starting from tomorrow.' He took Flora's hand in his, pinching her in warning, hoping the shock of the last five minutes had sobered her up. *Play along.*

To his relief she picked up his cue. 'Pleased to meet you. I am very excited to be working with you and to help breathe life and colour into Alex's designs. I didn't realise I would have the honour of meeting you this evening otherwise...' Flora gestured at her wrinkled dress, at her mussed-up hair '...I would have made more of an effort.'

'But no.' Camilla's face had relaxed—as much as her tightened skin would allow—into a smile. 'The apology is all mine. I should have warned you that I had changed my plans. I have interrupted your last evening of privacy.'

'Oh, no.' Flora's cheeks were pink and her hand hot in Alex's. 'Not at all, we have mostly been working...' Her voice trailed off at the knowing look on Camilla's face as she said the last word.

'It all looks absolutely fantastic, just as I envisioned.' Alex took over the conversation, taking pity on Flora. 'And the staff seem to know their roles perfectly—not that I would expect anything else from a Lusso Hotel. What time can we expect the guests tomorrow?'

Camilla accepted a glass of wine from a discreetly hovering waiter and sat down on one of the chairs by the stove. 'We're expecting the first to arrive after lunch tomorrow. I am so pleased you agreed to spend this opening week with us, Alex. The majority of the guests are influential travel journalists and bloggers and I am sure they are going to have lots of questions about your inspiration for this beautiful building. But please, not all work, eh? You must take full advantage of the facilities while you are here.'

Again she swept a knowing look up and down the pair of them. Alex gritted his teeth. 'It's my absolute pleasure. It's not often I get to spend so much time in a building I designed after completion. It will be really interesting to watch it fulfil its purpose.' Alex stole a glance at Flora. She was no longer flushed, rather she had turned pale, as if all the life had been leached out of her apart from the dark circles shadowing her eyes.

'However, if I'm to ensure the Bali designs are perfect for our meeting at the end of the week and socialise appropriately I think we'd better turn in. We were on the road at five a.m.'

'Of course. I look forward to seeing your designs, Miss Buckingham. Alex has been singing your praises. I can't wait to be impressed.'

Flora had thought she knew all about humiliation. She was the high priestess of it, dedicated to short sharp bursts at regular intervals. There was the awful day her university boyfriend announced he was in love with her sister; the even more awful day her subsequent boyfriend admitted he was in love with Alex; the time she thought her last boyfriend had been proposing when he had, in fact, been breaking up with her.

She had been going to refuse him, of course. But that *so* wasn't the point.

Her redundancy and the nasty smile on Finn's face as he had watched her gather up her pitifully small box of belongings and get escorted from the building like a thief.

Yep. High priestess of humiliation. Case in point: the week of catastrophes she had just experienced.

But, nope. None of them equalled the scene just now. She would rather sit on a hundred strange men's laps on any sort of public transport than relive the scene she had just left.

Flora squeezed her eyes shut as if she could block out the memory by will alone. *Kiss me, Alex.*

Oh, but he had. And it had been…it had been…

Flora flopped onto the bed and searched for the word. It had been wonderful. Right until the moment he had pushed her away with horror in his eyes and disgust on his face. That bit had sucked.

No. That had been the worst moment of her life. Bar none. Much, *much* worse than last time. At least she hadn't asked him, *begged* him to kiss her then. She'd just misjudged a moment. She should have learned her lesson. She wasn't what he wanted. Not in that way. Not then, not now.

She could never face him again. She should pack her bags and escape down the mountain, at night, in thick snow. She couldn't ski, didn't have a car and Innsbruck was several miles below. But that didn't matter, the exit plan itself mere details. The important thing was that she needed to escape and to pretend she had never ever laid eyes on Alex Fitzgerald with his crooked smile and red-brown curls.

But then he would spend Christmas alone. And without her family what did he have? He would never show it, of course, never say anything but she *knew*. She saw the look of relief when he stepped through the front door into her parents' hall. Saw him almost physically set down whatever burdens he carried around along with his overnight bag. Watched him relax, really relax, as he talked sport with Horatio—not that Horry had much of a clue but he tried to keep up. Watched the laughter lurk in his eyes as he half teased, half flirted with Minerva in a way no other mortal, not even her own husband, could get away with.

He helped her dad in the kitchen, talked through work problems with her mum and was on Flora's side. Always.

No, he couldn't be allowed to leave them. She would just have to grin, bear it and blame the schnapps. Not for the first time.

And she would work hard. She would blow the caramel-haired, caramel-clad, tight-skinned Camilla Lusso's designer socks off with her colour schemes, materials and designs. She would make Alex proud and this would be just a teeny footnote in their history. Never to be mentioned again. Never to be...

What now? A knock on the door interrupted her fervent vowing. Flora pushed herself off the bed, smoothed down her hair. *Please don't let it be Camilla Lusso.* There was no way she was ready for round two. 'Come in.'

A bellboy pushed the door open and smiled politely. 'Excuse me, Fraulein. I have Herr Fitzgerald's bags if now is convenient?'

If now was *what*?

'I beg your pardon?'

'Frau Lusso asked me to move Herr Fitzgerald's bags into your room.' He opened the door a little wider, pushing a trolley through heaped with Alex's distinctive brown leather bags.

'But…' Flora shook her head. Was she dreaming? Hallucinating? Had she been drinking absinthe? That would explain a lot. Maybe the whole hideous evening had been some weird absinthe-related dream.

'Mr Fitzgerald has his own room.'

'Not any more,' Alex stepped into the room, just behind the bellboy. His voice was light but there was a grim set to his face, his eyes narrowed as he stared at her. 'Camilla very kindly said there was no need for us to be discreet and we absolutely shouldn't spend the week before Christmas apart. Nice bath. Do you want first dibs or shall I?'

'You can't stay here.' Flora sank back onto the bed and stared at the pile of bags. It was most unfair; how did Alex have proper stuff? They were more or less the same age. How had he managed to turn into an actual functioning grown-up with matching luggage filled with the correct clothes for every occasion?

'What do you suggest?' He seemed unruffled as he opened up the first, neatly packed suitcase and began to lay his top-of-the-line ski kit out onto the other side of the bed.

'Well, we'll just say we're not ready for this step. Say we're waiting.'

'We're waiting?' An unholy glint appeared in his eye. 'How virtuous.'

'People do...' Her cheeks were hot and she couldn't look at him. All desire to discuss anything relating to love or sex or kissing with Alex Fitzgerald had evaporated the minute she had caught the disgust in his eyes. Again.

'They do,' he agreed, picking up his pile of clothes and disappearing into the walk-in wardrobe with them. 'Why haven't you unpacked?'

Flora blinked, a little stunned by his rapid turn of conversation. 'I have. Those clothes there? They're mine.'

'But where are your ski clothes? You can't hit the slopes in jeans.'

Flora winced. She had a suspicion that hitting would be the right verb if she did venture out on skis—as in her bottom repeatedly and painfully hitting the well-packed snow. 'I don't ski.'

Alex had reappeared and was shaking his tuxedo out of another of the bags; somehow it was miraculously uncreased. Another grown-up trick. 'Flora, we're here to mingle and promote the hotel. In winter it's a ski hotel. I don't think staying away from the slopes is optional. Did you pack anything for the dinners and the ball?'

The what? 'You didn't mention a ball.' Unwanted, hot tears were pricking at her eyes. Any minute he'd inform her that she needed to cook a cordon-bleu meal for sixty and she would win at being completely inadequate.

'You'll have to go shopping tomorrow. You need a ski outfit, another couple of formal dresses for dinner and something for the ball.'

Flora leaned forward and covered her face with her hands, trying to block the whole scene, the whole evening, the whole day out. If she wished hard enough then maybe it would all go away. She'd wake up and be back on the train, squashed onto the knee of a leering stranger, and she'd know that there were worse ways to make a fool of herself.

'I can't afford to go shopping for things I'll only wear once. I cut up my credit cards so I wouldn't be tempted to go into debt and until I get paid next Friday I have exactly two hundred and eight pounds in my account—and I need to live on next week's pay until I go back to London after New Year. We don't all have expense accounts and savings and disposable income.'

It was odd, arguing over clothes and money when so much had happened in the last half-hour. But in a way it was easier, far better to worry about the small stuff than the huge, shattering things.

'You're doing a job for me so you can use my expense account. We'll go into Innsbruck tomorrow morning.'

His tone suggested a complete lack of interest

in pursuing the subject. It just ramped up Flora's own annoyance.

'How very convenient.' She was going for icy hauteur but was horribly afraid she just sounded sulky. 'Typical Fitzgerald high-handedness.' She glared at him. 'Will you stop that, stop unpacking as if you are planning to stay here? Just say you need the space to work and there simply isn't the privacy in this room.' She cast a desperate look at the bath. She'd never dare use it now.

'I tried that and Camilla offered me her office. Look, Flora…' Alex put down the pile of jumpers and ran a hand through his hair. 'If we act like this is a problem then she'll get suspicious. I probably shouldn't have lied but I didn't want her to think badly of you. She's very strict on first impressions and professional behaviour from everyone she works with. You and I know that what happened didn't mean anything, it was just a silly moment that got out of hand…'

Whoosh. His words kicked Flora right in the stomach.

'But look at it from her point of view. It'll look

even worse if she thinks we lied. What's done is done, it's only a week.' He was so dismissive, as if this was no big deal. But then it wasn't a big deal for him, was it? 'I'll take the couch. Your virtue is safe with me.'

That was only too clear. Unfortunately.

'Come on.' He grabbed a pillow and a quilt from the wardrobe and took them over to the sofa. 'Let's grab some sleep. It was an early start and we've a busy day tomorrow. You can have first go in the bathroom and tomorrow…' He smiled but it didn't reach his eyes. 'Tomorrow we'll figure out a privacy rota for the bath.'

Flora might have got the bed rather than the low, modern, 'easy on the eye but far less easy on the body' sofa but that didn't make sleep any easier. She'd shared rooms with Alex before. Heck, she'd squeezed into a misleadingly named two-man tent with him many times at festivals. But tonight, hearing the slow, easy sounds of his breathing, sleep eluded her.

Flora was more aware of Alex than she had ever been before in her entire life. She had known him as a lanky, red-headed, freckled boy, sleeping on her floor in his striped boarding-school-approved pyjamas, crying out for his long-dead mother in his sleep. She had watched over him as he began to grow into those long limbs, as muscles formed in his shoulders and legs, as other girls began to cast covert—and not so covert—glances at him. And she had watched him learn to glance back.

But she didn't know him at all tonight.

And yet she couldn't stop sensing him. Sensing the strength in his arms, the artistry in the sensitive fingers. She knew without looking just how his jaw curved, how his hair fell over his forehead, how his eyes were shuttered, hiding his thoughts even from her. Especially from her. She felt every movement as if he were lying right next to her, not with what might as well be acres of polished floorboards between them.

She had to stop loving him once and for all or else she risked losing him for ever. And if she lost him then where would he go? Would he lose himself in short-term relationship after fling, trading one gazelle-like blonde for another as carelessly as if they were new shirts? This whole nightmare was a wake-up call. Alex was right. She had to grow up.

And grow out of loving him.

CHAPTER FOUR

IF ALEX EVER needed a new job then he could always audition for work as an actor. As long as the role demanded he was asleep throughout. He'd spent an entire night rehearsing for just such a role.

Lying still but not so still it seems unnatural? Check. Breathing deeply? Check. Resisting the temptation to add in the odd snore? Check. Playing word games, counting sheep and alpine cows and blades of grass? Oh, yes. Very much check.

Doing anything and everything to keep his mind away from the bed just a few feet away— and from the warm body occupying it? Check. Not dwelling in miserable detail on the long limbs, the tousled hair and the wide, sensual mouth just made for kissing? No, no check. He'd failed miserably.

It was all too reminiscent of his last summer

in his father's house. Lying in his bed at home during the long school holidays, wishing he were in the little attic room that Flora's family only half jokingly called his or even, on the worst nights, wishing he were back at school in the dorm room filled with the cheesy, musty scent of adolescent boys.

It wasn't as bad when his father was at home. Then he just had to listen to the noise. The drinking, the laughing, the noisy lovemaking. But his father was so seldom home.

He didn't know what was worse. The way he had dreaded the creak of the door when his stepmother came in to 'check on him'—or the way he had anticipated it. The musky smell of her shampoo. The way the bed dipped where she sat. The cool caress on his cheek. Her whisper. *'Alex, are you awake?'*

And so he had practised his breathing, kept his eyes lightly closed and pretended that he wasn't. He didn't think he ever had her fooled. And in the end she stopped asking if he was awake. Stopped waiting for permission.

In the end he had stopped pretending.

No. He rolled over, the narrow sofa uncomfortable beneath his hip. No. He mustn't think of his stepmother and Flora in the same way, at the same time. They were nothing alike. He couldn't, wouldn't taint Flora with that association. She was better than that. Better than him.

Far too good for him. He had always known that.

And that was why he had to step away. Just as he had all those years ago. He'd broken up his childhood home with his out-of-control desires. He'd been so lucky that Flora's family had stepped in and offered him a second home, an infinitely better home. He couldn't, absolutely couldn't let desire infiltrate that space. No matter what.

He opened one eye, relieved to see the room turning grey with the pre-dawn light. Slowly, stealthily he slid off the sofa, wincing as he straightened his legs; he felt like the princess must have after her night sleeping on a pea—if her bed had also been too narrow to allow her to turn and a good foot too short. He tiptoed to the door and slid it open. He could have sworn he heard a sigh of relief from Flora as the door slipped shut behind him.

He needed a run. He needed a swim. And most of all he needed a very long and very cold shower while he figured out just how he was going to survive the rest of the week.

'I hope you slept well?' Camilla smiled in welcome when Alex walked into the dining hall two hours later. Darn, he had hoped to have more time to gather his thoughts but it was too late. They were on. Time to be convincing.

'Like a baby,' he lied, searching for a subject that didn't involve sleep, Flora or the suite they were now sharing. 'Look at the morning light in here. It's spectacular.'

'It should be. You designed it that way.'

'That's true, I did.' And he had. But it was always an unexpected joy to see his dreams made real.

The hotel was on the western slopes facing

Innsbruck and so the huge windows were always most effective in the evening when the sun hung low in the evening sky and began to set. To counter this and to ensure the dining room didn't feel too dark during the day, Alex had designed it as a glassed-in roof terrace with dramatic skylights positioned to capture as much morning sun as possible. Balconies ran around the entire room so summer visitors could enjoy the warm Alpine sun as they ate.

Like the rest of the hotel the floor was a warm, golden oak, the same wood as the tables and chairs and the long counters that ran along one side. Guests could help themselves to juice, fruit and a continental breakfast; discreetly hovering staff were there to take orders for hot breakfasts. There was no menu; the kitchen was prepared for most requests.

Alex strolled over to the counter and poured himself some orange juice before spooning fresh berries into a bowl. 'Coffee, please.' He smiled at the hovering waitress. 'And scrambled eggs, on rye bread. That's all, thanks.'

He took his fruit and drink over to the square table where Camilla sat, basking in the sunlight like a cat. Her plate was bare and she had a single espresso set in front of her. In the two years they had worked together Alex had never seen her eat. He suspected she ran off caffeine, wine and, possibly, the blood of young virgins.

Camilla took a dainty sip of her espresso. 'I think I made the right call on the mattresses. I know they were expensive, but a hotel like this needs the best, hmm?'

Alex nodded, wishing he had had the opportunity to sample the mattress himself. 'Of course. Your guests wouldn't settle for anything less.'

Camilla eyed him shrewdly. 'A hotel tracksuit? Very good of you to live the brand, Alex.'

He speared a blueberry on a fork. 'Early morning workout. I didn't want to wake Flora. Good idea to have them where anyone could borrow them. I wonder how many people will slip one into their suitcase?'

She shrugged dismissively. 'Let them. They pay enough—and it's all good branding.' She looked over at the door. 'Good morning, Miss Buckingham.'

'Good morning.' Flora wandered over to the table, a glass of juice in her hand. Alex gave her a quick critical look. She had on more make-up than usual, as if she was trying to conceal the dark shadows under her eyes. It might fool anyone who didn't know her. It didn't fool him for a second.

Had she been pretending to sleep as well?

A little belatedly Alex remembered his role as adoring lover and got to his feet to give her a brief peck on the cheek. He closed his eyes for a brief second as her warm, comforting scent enfolded him. 'Morning.'

Her eyes flew to his. He couldn't read her expression at all. He expected anger, discomfort maybe. Instead all he saw was determination.

Interesting—and very unexpected. She looked different too. Her dark hair pulled back into a loose bun, the dark green tunic belted over her jeans not left to hang shapelessly. She'd accessorised the whole with a chunky silver bead necklace and earrings. She looked smarter, more together.

And, yep, she looked determined. For what he wasn't entirely sure.

'I need to go into Innsbruck this morning,' Flora said after giving her breakfast order to the waitress. Alex's coffee arrived as she did so and he gratefully poured a cup of the delicious, dark, caffeinated nectar, offering it to Flora before pouring his own.

It was all very domesticated.

'I only brought work clothes. I didn't realise that I would be participating in the week's activities.' She smiled over at Alex. 'Apparently I won't be able to avoid learning to ski any longer although I'm sure I'd be far more useful concentrating on all the lovely après-ski activities.'

Camilla drained her cup. 'I think learning to ski is an excellent idea. You really should look at the hotel's ski lodges. I'd be interested to hear what you think of the materials and colours. They're accessible by ski lift but the only way back down the mountain is on the slopes.'

Flora grimaced. 'I can't wait to see them but I have to admit I'm a little nervous about the whole "two bits of plastic on snow" part. I can ice skate but other than that my balance is decidedly wonky. But hey, *carpe diem* and all that. It's good to try new things.'

Alex looked up. What was going on with her? Something was definitely different. Her tone, the way she was dressed. Did this have anything to do with yesterday? Their disagreement—or what happened later?

He should step back. This was what he wanted for her, right? For Flora to be more confident, to start living. And he could do with his space too. To make sure he cleared any lingering sentiments from that darned kiss from his system so they could go back to being easy with each other.

He looked out of the window. It was a glorious day, the sun already high in the blue winter's sky, lighting up the snowy peaks in brilliant colour. He should stay in and work—but the contrast to the damp fog he had left behind in London was almost painful. He yearned to get out, to clear his lungs and his mind in the cold, clear air.

Besides, Flora had never skied before; she had no idea what she needed—an easy target for anyone wanting to hit their sales targets. And it *was* his company's expense account on the line. 'I'll come in with you. Unless I'm needed here, Camilla?'

'No, no.' His client shook her head. 'You have a lovely day. Visit the Christmas markets and enjoy Innsbruck. I'll be doing the tour of the hotel when the guests arrive. I don't need you for that. This evening I am planning a mulled-wine reception and sledge rides for my guests. It would be nice if you were here for the reception so that I can introduce you.'

'Absolutely. Sounds great.'

Flora didn't say anything while Camilla sat with them but as soon as she sauntered away Flora pushed her plate away and narrowed her eyes at Alex. 'I don't need a chaperone. I hate shopping enough as it is. The last thing I want is you hanging around looking bored.'

'I love shopping,' he promised her, reaching over and nicking a small Danish pastry from her plate. 'Don't worry about me. I'll be absolutely fine.'

She smacked his hand as he carried the pastry away. 'I wasn't worrying about *you*. I'm going to try out the swimming pool first while I can be sure of having it to myself if you want to go and get changed.' Her cheeks flushed pink and she avoided his eyes. 'I'll be at least an hour so you have plenty of time to, you know… Change.'

He did know. She didn't want to walk in on him. Last summer when they had shared a tent at the festival she'd been content to stand outside the tent flap and yell an imperious demand to know whether he was decent or not. Those more innocent days were gone, maybe irrevocably. He tried for a light humour. 'We should have a code. Like college students—a ribbon on the door handle means don't come in.'

'I'd be tempted to keep one on there all the time.' But she smiled as she said it, a welcome attempt at the old easy camaraderie. 'I'll see you in the foyer at around eleven. You bring the credit cards and arms ready to carry lots of bags. I'll just bring me.'

It was annoying. She was annoying. Annoying and pitiful. Annoying, pitiful and pathetic. Yep, that just about covered it. Flora grimaced at herself in the half-steamed-up changing-room mirror. She shouldn't be glad that he wanted to spend the day with her. She should tell him to stick his pretend relationship and his begrudging job offer and his expense account—and then she should go spend the day sightseeing before jumping back onto a plane and heading home to re-evaluate her life.

All of it.

But instead she was taking extra care drying her hair and reapplying the make-up she had swum off—and not just because this wide room, tiled in bronze and cream, was the most comfortable and well equipped changing room she had ever set foot in. It was going to be very difficult going back to her local council gym with its uncomfortable shared changing facilities and mouldy grout after the thick towels, rainforest showers and cushioned benches.

No, she couldn't deny it; she was looking forward to the day ahead. Because when all was said and done he was still Alex Fitzgerald and she was still Flora Buckingham. Life-long best mates, blood brothers and confidants and surely one embarrassing drunken episode and one insanely hot kiss couldn't change that.

She wouldn't let it change that.

And she wasn't going to sulk and dwell on his words from the previous afternoon either. Flora's hands stilled as shame shot through her, sharp and hot. He knew her too well, knew how to hit a tender spot, how to pierce right through the armour of denial she had been building up. She was too afraid of messing up. So scared of getting it wrong that she had ignored her instincts and selected purely science A levels in a bid to show her parents that she was as clever as her brother, as her Oxford-educated, high-flying sister.

But in the end what had she proved? Nothing. Quitting her vet course might have been the right thing to do but in the end it had just confirmed all their ideas. That she wasn't quite as robust as the rest of her family, not quite as determined.

Flora resumed drying her hair. For once it was going right, the frizz tamed, the curls softened into waves. Maybe this was a good omen for the weeks ahead. The truth was even now she wasn't sure she knew what she *really* wanted, deep down inside. Was she so determined to find more work as an in-house designer simply because that was easiest, hiding behind somebody else's brief, somebody else's brand? Or should she be trying to step away from the corporate world and indulge what he called her *whimsy*?

The little designs she played with might indeed be whimsical, fantastical even, but they had their fans. After all, her little online shop selling scarves and cushion covers in her designs ticked over nicely. Imagine how it would do if she actually gave it all her attention.

She smoothed some gorgeous-smelling oil onto

her hair and twisted it back into the loose bun. Three hotels, three design briefs. This could buy her the time and income she needed to find out where her heart lay. Or was she going to wander from dream to dream for ever, never quite committing? Always afraid of failing. Of falling.

No. This week was a wake-up call in all kinds of ways. And she was going to make the most of it.

She smiled her thanks at the chambermaid who was already collecting her towels and returning the changing room into its pristine state ready to wow the expected guests. Flora knew that along with the journalists and bloggers a few influential winter-sports fanatics had been invited; a couple of ex-Olympians and several trust-fund babies. They would expect only the best even from a free jolly like this one and Camilla and her staff were determined they would get it.

Maybe that could be her career? Travelling from luxury hotel to luxury hotel to be pampered and indulged in the hope that she would say something nice about it. How long would it take to get bored of that? She was more than willing to find out.

She wandered up the stairs to the large, high-ceilinged foyer. It would be the first impression of the hotel for all future guests and so it had to set the standard: light, spacious, with quality in every fitting. Would the people expected here later notice—or did they take such attention to detail for granted? It would be nice to be that jaded…

Yes. Nice was the word. Although she was a long, long way from jaded. Driven into Innsbruck, attentive service in all the shops and, best of all, the hotel driver stayed ready to collect her bags and whisk them back. If only she'd been buying something useful like fabric rather than over-priced, over-stuffed shiny clothes.

'I could get used to this,' Flora confided, watching her bags get loaded into the small hotel city car, ready to be delivered back to her room—their room—and hung up ready for her return. 'I think I was always made to be part of the other half.'

'It's not the other half,' Alex pointed out. 'It's the other one per cent and, I don't know, I think it would do them good to carry their own bags some of the time.'

'Don't spoil my fairy tale. Expense accounts and my every whim taken care of? I feel like a Christmas Cinderella.'

'And who am I? Buttons?'

He hadn't cast himself as Prince Charming. Flora ignored the stab of disappointment and linked arms with him, just as she usually would. *Act normal, remember?* Alex gave a barely susceptible start before falling into step with her.

'No,' she said sweetly. 'You are my fairy godmother. I can just see you in pink tulle.'

He spluttered a surprised bark of laughter and despite herself her heart lifted. They could get back on track even if they did have to share a room. As long as neither of them used that darned bathtub. It had been the first thing she had seen when she opened her eyes that morning, taunting her with its suggestion of decadence.

'I don't remember the fairy godmother having such a hard time convincing Cinders to try on clothes.'

'That's because she wasn't making Cinders wear clothes that made her arse look huge, her bosom matronly and her hips look capable of bearing triplets. Ski clothes and curves do not mix. In fact, winter clothes and curves don't mix.' She had allowed Alex—or rather Alex's firm—to buy her the thermal turtle neck and leggings, the waterproof padded trousers and jacket, the fleece neck warmer, hat and gloves but had felt the whole time like a tomboy toddler being forced into a frilly bridesmaid dress. At least she had talked him out of the hot pink and gone for a less garish turquoise and white look. But she was pretty sure she'd still look and feel like a child playing dress up.

At least she was fairly happy with the dresses she had bought, even the formal dress for the ball. Actually, if she was honest with herself, she was secretly delighted with it—although whether she'd actually have the courage to wear it in public was a whole other matter. The sales assistants had been enthusiastic but then again that was their job. Just look how gushing the saleswoman had been when she had tried on the Bavarian-barmaid-inspired bridesmaid dress for Minerva's wedding. Even her father hadn't been able to summon up a heartfelt compliment for that particular outfit.

A little part of her wished she hadn't sent Alex away for what he rather insultingly called 'a restorative coffee' when she had started dress shopping, But it had been bad enough having him there assessing her while she tried on padded trousers. The thought of his eyes skimming over her in dress after dress was far too uncomfortable an image.

Innsbruck had no shortage of designer boutiques and stores but Flora had felt even more out of place in them than she had in the bustling board shops. It had been such a relief when she had stumbled on the vintage shop with floors and floors of second-hand and reproduction clothes. Usually she felt too self-conscious to wear anything that drew attention to herself—and with her height vintage always made a statement—but in this town of winter glamour it had been a choice between vintage inspired or designer glitz. No choice at all.

And it *was* a glamorous town. The old, medieval streets surrounded by snow-capped mountains gave Innsbruck a quaint, old-fashioned air but there was a cosmopolitan beat to the old Tyrolean town. People came here to shop at the Christmas markets and to enjoy the myriad winter sports aimed at all levels. There was a palpable sense of money, of entitlement, of health and vigour.

'Look at them all.' Flora stared down the main street at what seemed like a sea of glowing, youthful faces. 'It's like they've been ordered out of a catalogue. I've never seen so many gorgeous people.'

'Even him?' Alex indicated a man sitting in the window of a café, his sunglasses perched high on his unnaturally smooth face, his skin the colour of a ripened orange. Flora bit her lip, trying not to laugh.

'Or her?' He nudged her in the direction of a skeletally thin woman, swathed from neck to ankle in what Flora devoutly hoped were fake furs, incongruously bright yellow hair topping her wrinkled face.

'Maybe not everyone,' she conceded. 'But most people seem so at home, like they *belong*.' No one else bulged out of quilted jackets, or had hair flattened by their hats. The girls looked wholesomely winsome in thick jumpers and gilets, their hair cascading from underneath their knitted hats, their cheeks pink from the cold. The men were like Norse gods: tall, confident as they strode down the snow-filled medieval streets. Alex fitted the scene like the last piece of a jigsaw. Flora? She was the missing piece from a different jigsaw that had somehow got put in the wrong box.

'What did I tell you, Flora? No one really belongs, they just act like they do. You just need to stand tall and look people in the eye.'

'Not easy when everyone is wearing shades.' It was a feeble joke and Alex just looked at her, concern in his eyes. She winced; somehow she had managed to provoke almost every response going in the last forty-eight hours. She made herself smile. *See, joking.*

'We don't have to be back at the hotel for a few hours yet, you're respectably kitted out and I have even managed to clear my emails while you were dress hunting. What do you fancy doing?'

Flora pulled at her coat. 'I should work. What if Camilla wants to see my ideas? All I have are a few online mood boards.'

'That's all she wants at this stage. I can promise you, she'll change her mind a million times and in the end your first concept will be the winner.'

'Then why drag me here for the week?' Oh, no. He hadn't forced her over here as some sort of intervention, had he? He could just imagine him on the phone to her mother, reassuring her that he had it all in hand. That he would put an end to this temping nonsense quick smart.

'Not that I'm not grateful…' she added unconvincingly. Just think, if he'd left her alone she could have been cosying up to the man on the train again tomorrow morning. Maybe she'd misjudged him and his grabby hands. He might just be plain-speaking and tactile. They could have told their kids and grandkids about how they'd met on an overcrowded commuter train a week before Christmas. Just like a film.

'Flora, Camilla can snap her fingers and have the best at the touch of a button. It's the story, the package that she needs to see. She loves that I'm young, terribly English, well educated, have my own firm and I'm tipped for the top.' His laugh was a little self-conscious. 'It's an easy sell, makes a good interview, adds that extra little detail when she's publicising the hotel. You're here so she can see that you can do the same—that's why it's so important that you look right, that you say the right things.'

That she what? Panic churned in her stomach,

the snow dazzling as she stared at the ground, her eyes swimming. 'I'm here to schmooze? You didn't tell me that!'

'I didn't hide it. You know who the invited guests are. Look, Camilla knows I wouldn't recommend anyone who wasn't talented and creative. She needs to see that you can mingle with the right people, chat to journalists, help sell her creations. And, Flora, you can.'

'But I can't...' He wanted her to what? *Chat to journalists? Sell?* Flora gulped in air, rooted to the spot, oblivious to the crowds passing her by.

'You've done it before.' He didn't add *Many times* but the words hung in the air. 'At least this time you won't have to baste chickens or pipe icing while you're talking.'

Flora still couldn't joke about her childhood spots in front of the camera. To be honest she wasn't sure she ever would reach that state. 'Can you imagine what it was like going into school after Dad's shows aired? Me this tall and this...' She sketched an arc around her chest. She had been the tallest in her class from nursery onwards—and the most developed from the end of primary school. 'The last thing I want to do is talk about me, you know that. And if I chat to journalists they'll know who I am…'

'And they'll love it. Youngest daughter of food writer and TV chef, Ted Buckingham and TV doctor Jane Buckingham? They won't try and catch you out, Flora. We're talking travel sections, maybe some lifestyle blogs. I promise you. It'll be a lot less stressful than your dad's Internet videos of family get-togethers.'

'Horry says neurosurgery is less stressful than the Internet get-togethers.'

'All you have to do this week is have fun. Try to ski, chat to people, talk colours and materials and be enthusiastic. If Camilla offers you the commission then you can worry about the other side of it later, but if I were you I'd think about how a little publicity in the right places could send your stock sky-high. Come on, Flora. You never know, you might even enjoy it. Now, Christmas markets or ice skating? Your choice.'

Flora took in a deep shuddering breath. Alex

was right, if he'd mentioned any of this before she would have hightailed it back to London before he could say *prost*. Minerva positively fed off their parents' fame, using it as a springboard when she opened her PR firm, and Horry was oblivious. Flora, on the other hand, had always found it mortifying, whether appearing on her dad's cookery programme or listening to her mother talk about Flora's first period on national TV. She wasn't sure the scars from that particular episode would ever fade.

Still, silver linings and all that—she hadn't thought about the kiss or their sleeping arrangements once in the last half-hour. It turned out there were only so many things even she could stress about.

'I haven't been ice skating for years.'

'Indoors or outdoors?'

Flora looked around, at the blue sky, the sun warm despite the chill of the air. 'Oh, outside, please.'

'Come on, then, I challenge you to a backwards-skating race. Loser buys the mulled wine.'

CHAPTER FIVE

THIS WHOLE WEEK was doomed. Alex had known it from the minute he'd got Lola's email. Camilla Lusso liked to work with people she could show off. Extroverted, larger than life, Lola had fitted the bill perfectly. Flora? Not so much. But she did have the training, after all. It wasn't as if he had thrown her in unprepared; she'd been brought up with camera crews, journalists and interviewers traipsing through the house, had been expected to converse intelligently at dinner parties and receptions since she'd hit double figures.

Of course, that didn't mean she *enjoyed* any of it. Alex knew all too well that if he'd been completely honest with her at the start she'd have run a mile.

Maybe that would have been for the best. No Flora, no kiss, no sleepless night.

Because, try as he might, he just couldn't shake the memory of the warmth of her mouth, the sweetness of her lips, the way his hands had held her as if she were made just for him, every curve slotting so perfectly against him.

There had been far too many kisses from far more women than Alex cared to remember. Not one had stayed with him, not for a second. This one he could still taste. He had a feeling he would still feel it imprinted on his lips in fifty years' time.

And it was all he could do not to put his hands on her shoulders, turn her around and kiss her once again. And this time there would be no stepping back. Not ever.

But he couldn't. She deserved better than him. She needed someone who wasn't dead inside, someone who could match her sweetness and generous spirit. Sometimes Alex thought that Flora could be the saving of him—but he'd be the damning of her. His father's last words echoed around his brain yet again.

You taint everything you touch. You were born bad and grew up worse.

And his father was right.

But he wouldn't taint Flora, never Flora.

'I haven't been ice skating in years.' She worried away at her lower lip as they walked through the twisty streets. 'Not since we used to go to the ice discos on a Friday night. Not that you did much skating. You were usually in a corner snogging some random girl.'

He had been. A different girl each week. The worse he'd behaved, the more they'd seemed to find him irresistible. He had hated himself every single Friday night as he'd smiled across at yet another hopeful—but it hadn't stopped him moving in while last week's conquest had watched from a corner.

Had anything changed? He went in for relationships now, not kisses in a booth by an ice rink, but he didn't commit as much as a toothbrush to them—and Flora had a point when she said that each of his girlfriends was interchangeable. A warm body to lose himself in, a talisman against the dark.

Could he change that—did he even want to?

Or would it be just as lonely with one woman by his side as it was with dozens?

He shook off the thought. 'It'll be just like riding a bike—the skating, not the snogging.' Why had he said that? He was pretty sure that the red in her cheeks had nothing to do with the cold and she ducked her head so that he couldn't see her expression.

It'll get easier, he told himself. But he hoped it was soon. He couldn't imagine being this awkward in front of her parents. He knew Flora thought they favoured him but there was no contest—she was their little girl and if he hurt her they'd take her side. As they should.

It made him aware just how alone he was in the world. Was there anyone who would be on his side no matter what?

There were lots of ice rinks in and around Innsbruck, the prettiest on naturally frozen lakes, but the one Alex had chosen had a charm all of its own. It was a temporary rink right in the centre of town, just a short walk from the bustling Christmas markets. The early afternoon sun was too bright for the Christmas lights hanging overhead and bedecking every tree to make any impact but Alex knew that once dusk fell the whole town would light up, a dazzling, golden winter wonderland of crystal and light.

The rink was busy and it took a while before they could pay and order their skates. The boots were tight and stiff, unfamiliar on his feet, a reminder as he awkwardly stood up just how long it was since he had last been skating. Judging by Flora's awkward gait, she felt the same way. Gingerly they walked, stiff-legged and heavy-footed, to the wide entrance and peered at the whirling crowd. Even the toddlers seemed to have a professional air as they flew round and round, their mittened hands clasped behind their backs.

Alex grimaced. 'I'm not sure about that backward race; right now just going forwards feels like it might be a struggle.'

Flora slid her foot forward, wobbling like a fawn who had only just found her feet, her arms windmilling madly as she found her balance.

'Come on, we just need to find our feet. It'll be fine. I used to be able to dance on the ice.'

'Synchronised moves to pop. It wasn't exactly figure skating,' he pointed out as he put a tentative toe on the white surface, his eyes following a slight figure who did seem to be practising figure skating as she looped elegant circles round and round. 'I don't think we ever got to Austrian standards.'

Flora slid out another cautious foot and then another, a smile playing around her mouth as she began to pick up speed. 'Speak for yourself! You should have spent more time skating, less time being the local Casanova,' she yelled over her shoulder as she struck out for the centre of the rectangular rink.

Alex took a quick look around. On the far side the tented café was open to the rink and filled with cheerful onlookers clutching hot drinks and waving at family members as they skated close. At both ends spectators paused in their shopping to watch the sport. Christmas music blared from

speakers and a giant, lit-up Christmas tree occupied the very centre of the rink.

He could stay here, clinging to the handrail, or
he could venture out. Come on, he used to spend
every weekend doing this. His body must remember the moves. Grimly he let go and began
to move.

That was it, knees bent, body weight forward,
letting the blades cut at an angle and propel him
forward. The air chilled on his face as he got
up some speed, the rest of his body warming
with the exertion. Where was Flora? Squinting
through a gang of teens, arms locked as they
swung round in matching step, he saw her,
weaving nimbly in and out of the other skat-
ers. He'd always liked to watch her on the ice.
She lost all self-consciousness, graceful as she
pirouetted around.

She saw him and skated an elegant figure of
eight, the ice swishing under her skates as she
pulled up alongside him.

'Hey.' She smiled at him, any trace of reserve

gone in the wide beam. 'This is brilliant. Why don't we do this any more?'

'Because we're not sixteen?'

'That's a rubbish reason. Look, there are plenty of people here way older than us.'

'And way younger.' Alex nodded towards one of the toddler prodigies and Flora laughed.

'He must have been born with skates on. Come on, let's go faster…'

She grabbed his hand and struck out and with a shout of alarm mixed with exultation he joined her, their gloved hands entwined, their bodies moving in swift, perfect synchronicity as they whirled faster and faster and faster round and round and round. All he could hear was his blood pumping in his ears, the roar of the wind and the beat of the music; colours swirled together as they moved past, through and round other groups until someone's foot, he wasn't sure whose, slipped and they crashed together, a sliding, flailing, unbalancing. Somehow he managed to grab hold of Flora and steady her before she fell completely onto the ice and they backed carefully to the side, holding onto each other, laughing.

'That was brilliant.' Her eyes shone, her cheeks were pink with exertion and her breath came in pants. She had never looked more magnificent, like some winter naiad glorying in the ice.

'Yes.' He wanted to say more but all the words had gone. All he could see were her long lashes, tipped with snow, her wide laughing mouth, a mouth made for kissing. All he could feel was her softness, nestled in next to him.

He had held her before, stood this close to her before. If he was honest he had wanted her before. But he'd hidden it, even from himself, every single time before. It was as if yesterday's kiss had opened the gates, shown him the forbidden fruit concealed behind them and now that he had tasted he wasn't sure he could ever stop craving.

It was a bad idea. But God help him he'd forgotten why. And when she looked at him like that, tentative, hopeful, naked desire blazing from those dark, dark eyes, he was utterly undone.

It was a bad idea. But Alex pushed that thought away as the air stilled, as the beat of the music faded away replaced with the thrum of need beating its own time through his veins, through his blood. He stood, drinking her in like a dying man at an oasis. All he had to do was bend his head…

He paused, allowing the intoxicating possibility to fill him—and then he stood back. 'Come on.' His voice was rough, rasping like yesterday's beard. 'We need to get back.'

It was a bad idea. If only it didn't feel so wickedly, seductively good. If only doing the right thing didn't rip his heart right out of his chest.

He turned and skated away. And didn't look back once.

He'd nearly kissed her. She knew it completely. She'd seen it as his eyes had darkened to a stormy grey, as his breath had hitched and a muscle had pulsed on his cheek. She'd felt it as his arm had tightened around her shoulders, as her body had swayed into his. She hadn't thrown herself at him; she couldn't blame the schnapps, not this time.

No, Alex Fitzgerald had looked at her as if she were his last hope.

Of course, then he had turned and skated away as if all the Furies were chasing him down, but still. They had had a definite moment.

Which was pretty inconvenient because hadn't she vowed that this was it and she was going to Get Over Him no matter what? And then he had to go and look at her like that and all her good intentions were trampled into the ground like yesterday's snowfall.

Because that look went beyond mere lust. It *did*. It wasn't just wishful thinking. No, she had felt it penetrate right through to the core of her.

Flora sighed and nudged the hot tap with her foot and let another fall of steaming water into the tub. It felt decadently wrong to lie naked in the middle of such a big room, wearing just hot water and scented oils. The view from the bath-tub might be incredible but it seemed, a little disconcertingly, as if she were bathing right outside in the middle of a mountain glade.

Still, it was pretty relaxing—as long as Alex stuck to his timetable and didn't walk back in.

What if he did? Would he look like that again or would he back away terrified again?

Something was going on. *I need answers,* she decided, allowing herself to slip deep into the hot, almost to the point of discomfort, luxuriantly smelling water. She couldn't go on like this.

It was one thing thinking he was indifferent; horrid to think he was repulsed. But now? She had no idea. It was as if she were sixteen again. His face had that same remote, shuttered look it had worn all that long, hot summer.

She couldn't let him slip back to that place, wherever it was. She had been too shy, too unsure to ask questions then, to demand answers.

But maybe he needed her to ask them? Maybe by letting whatever had happened lie festering all these years she had done him a disservice. It didn't mean he would end up declaring his undying love for her, she knew that. It might change things for ever. But if she loved him then she needed to be strong, for once in her life. No matter what the personal cost.

And she wouldn't get anywhere lying in this bath, tempting as it was to stay in here all night long.

Although she wanted to try out one of the dresses she had bought that day, the prospect of a potential sledge ride made her think again and in the end Flora opted for her smartest black skinny jeans and a long, soft grey jumper with a snowflake motif. She started to automatically twist her hair into a ponytail but instead she let it flow freely across her shoulders, thankful that the wave had held and it hadn't been too flattened by the hat.

She stood before the mirror and looked down at the last purchase of the day, an impulse buy urged upon her by the shop assistants in the vintage shop. There was no way, they told her, that she could team her formal dress with her usual, insipid shade of lipstick.

She untwisted the top and stared down at the deep, dark red. A colour like that would only draw attention to her mouth and Flora had done her best to disguise its width since the day she had bought her first make-up. It had been the first thing she had been teased about—the kids at school had called her the wide-mouthed frog until she'd started to develop. The names after that had been cruder and even less original.

A sigh escaped her. It was just a colour. And nobody here knew her, would think twice about what colour she chose to paint her mouth. That was it, no more thought. She raised the small stick and quickly dabbed it across her lips, blending in the deep, rich colour. Then before she could backtrack and wipe it off again she turned on her heel and walked away from the mirror. No more hiding.

'This one seems to be ours.' Alex reached out and helped Flora into the old-fashioned, wooden sleigh. She climbed up carefully and settled herself onto the padded bench, drawing the fleecy blankets closely round herself, her feet thankful for the hot bricks placed on the floor. 'Four horses? They must have heard about the six cakes you put away during *Kaffee* and *Kuchen*.'

'At least I stuck to single figures,' she countered as he swung himself in beside her. Very close bedside her. Flora narrowed her eyes as she tried to make out the other sledges, already sliding away into the dark in a trample of hooves and a ringing of bells. Were they all so intimately small?

The driver shook the reins, causing a cascade of bells to ring out jauntily, and the sledge moved forward. She was all too aware of Alex's knee jammed tight against hers, his shoulders, his arm. The smell of him; like trees in spring and freshly cut grass, the scent incongruous in the dark of winter.

'Have you had a good time at the reception?' He was as formal as a blind date. It was the first time they had spoken this evening, the first interaction since she had taken a long deep breath and walked into the buzzing lounge. To her surprised relief the reception had been a lot less terrifying than she had anticipated. It was informal, although waitresses circled with glasses of mulled wine, spiced hot-chocolate rum and small, spicy canapés, and most people were more than happy to introduce themselves. The vibe was very much anticipatory and relaxed—the whole hotel felt very different, felt alive now that it was filled. It was no longer their private domain.

'You know, I actually have.' She turned and smiled at him. 'I had a lovely chat to Holly, she writes travel blogs and articles. Did you know her parents are journalists too? Her mum writes one of those family confessional weekly columns and Holly spent her whole childhood being mercilessly exposed in print as well!'

'That's great. I can see why you're so thrilled for her.'

'Obviously not great for *her*,' Flora conceded. 'But it was so nice to meet someone who understands just how mortifying it is. Her mum still writes about her—only now it's all about how she wishes she would stop travelling, settle down and pop out grandkids. At least mine hasn't gone there—yet.'

'No, but leave it more than five years and she might do a whole show about women who leave it too late to have babies.' His mouth quirked into a wicked smile.

'If she does I'll get her to do a companion show about aging sperm count and use *you* as her patient,' Flora countered sweetly and was rewarded by an embarrassed cough.

Silence fell, a silence as dark and impenetrable as the night sky. They were both sitting as far apart as possible, almost clinging onto the side rails, but it was no good; every move of the sleigh slid them back along the narrow bench until they were touching again.

It was all too horribly, awkwardly, toe-curlingly romantic. From the sleigh bells tinkling as the proud-necked white horses trotted along the snowy tracks, to the lanterns the hotel had thoughtfully placed along the paths, the whole scenario was just begging for the lucky passengers to snuggle up under the thick blankets and indulge in some romance beneath the breathtakingly starry sky.

Or, alternatively, they could sit as far apart as possible and make the kind of stilted small talk that only two people who very much didn't want to be romantic could make. Remarks like, 'Look, aren't the stars bright?' and, 'The mountains are pretty.' Yep, Flora reflected after she had ventured a sentence about the height of the pine trees that stretched high up the mountainside, they were definitely reaching new depths of inanity.

If things were normal then they would be curled up laughing under the blankets. She would tease him about the women who had been clustered around him at the reception; he would try and cajole her to be a little more open-minded about her first ski lesson. They would probably refresh themselves from a hip flask. Completely at ease. But tonight the memory of that almost-kiss hung over them. It was in the clip clop of the horse's hooves, in the gasp of the sharp, cold mountain air, in the tall ghostly shadows cast by the lantern-lit trees.

'I feel like I should apologise,' she said after a while. 'And I *am* sorry for being drunk and silly, for putting you in a difficult position with Camilla. I am really sorry that you are having to sleep on the narrowest, most uncomfortable sofa I have ever had the misfortune to sit on in my life. And I'm sorry I kissed you.' She swallowed. 'I should have taken the hint when you stopped me all those years ago. But I've wanted to know what we'd be like most of my life. And when you told me I couldn't live in fear of rejection I just had to try, one more time...'

'And?' His voice was husky, as if it hurt him to speak. 'Was it worth it?'

'You tell me.' Flora shifted so she was sitting side on, so that she could see the inscrutable profile silhouetted against the dark night by the lantern light. 'Because I think actually that you wanted to as well. Maybe you have always wanted to. Even back then.'

He didn't answer for a long moment. Flora's

heart speeded up with every second of silence until she felt as if it might explode open with a bang.

'You're right. I did. And it was…it was incredible. But you and me, Flora. It would never work. You know that, right?'

Her heart had soared with the word incredible, only to plummet like an out-of-control ski jumper as he finished speaking.

She wasn't good enough for him. Just as she had always known. 'Because I don't have aspirations?' she whispered. 'Because I mess up?'

'No! It's not you at all.'

The denial only served to irritate her. Did he think she was stupid? 'Come on, Alex. I expected better from you of all people. You don't have to want me, it's okay, but please respect me enough not to fob me off with the whole "It's not you, it's me" line. Do you know how many times I've heard it? And I know *you* trot it out on a regular basis.'

'But this time I mean it. Dammit, Flora. Do you really think I'm good enough for you? That there's anything in my soulless, workaholic, shallow life that could make you happy?'

'I...' Was that really what he thought? 'You do make me happy. You're my best friend.'

'And you're mine and, believe me, Flora, I am more grateful for that than you will ever know. But you've been saving me since you were eight. Now it's my turn to save you. From me. Don't you think I haven't thought about it? How easy it would be? You're beautiful and funny and we fit. We fit so well. But you deserve someone whole. And I haven't been whole for a long, long time.'

How could she answer that? How could she press further when his voice was bleak and the look in his eyes, when the lamp highlighted them, was desolate? She took in a deep breath, the cold air sharpening her focus, the icy breeze freezing the tears that threatened to fall.

'I break everything I touch, Flora,' Alex said after a while. 'I can't, I won't break you. I won't break us. Because if I didn't have you in my life I wouldn't have anything. And I'm just too selfish to risk that.'

What about me? she wanted to ask. Don't I get a say? But she didn't say anything. Instead she slipped her glove off and reached her hand across until she found his, looping her cold fingers through his, anchoring him tightly. 'I'm not going anywhere,' she whispered, her head on his shoulder, breathing him in. 'I promise, you don't get rid of me that easily.'

He didn't answer but she felt the rigid shoulder relax, just a little, and his fingers clasped hers as if he would never let her go. Maybe this would be enough. It would have to be enough because it was all he was offering her.

CHAPTER SIX

'YOU ARE NOT seriously expecting me to get down there?' Flora pushed up her goggles and glared at the ski instructor.

He shrugged. 'It's the only way down.'

'Yes, but I thought we would stay on the nursery slopes until I could actually ski! This is a proper mountain. With snow on it.'

'Flora, you were too good for those within an hour and you nailed that blue. You are more than ready for this. Come on, it's an easy red. End the day on a high note.'

'Red!' She stared down the icy slope. Easy? It was practically vertical. Her palms dampened at the thought of launching her body down there. She glared at a small group of schoolkids as they enthusiastically pushed off. They were smaller, more compact. Had a lot less further to fall…

A figure skied easily down the higher slopes

towards them and pulled up with a stylish turn, which made Flora yearn to push them right over.

'Having trouble?' Alex. Of course. He was annoyingly at home on the slopes. Although, she reflected, he had an unfair disadvantage; after all he'd gone skiing with his school every year since he was eight. After he had left home and put himself through college and then university, his one extravagance was skiing holidays—although a host of rich school friends with their own chalets helped keep the costs down.

'She won't go,' her instructor explained. 'I tell her it's more than doable but she refuses.'

'So how are you planning to get down, Flora? Bottom first?'

She glared at the two of them, hating their identical, idiotic male grins. If only this particular slope had a nice cable car, like the one that had brought them up to the nursery slopes from the hotel. Then she could have just hopped back in and had a return ride. But no, it was a one way trip up in the lift and no way back down apart from on two plastic sticks.

Or she could wait here until spring and walk down in a nice sensible fashion.

The surprising thing was that she *had* been doing okay, that was very true. Surprisingly okay in fact. But not so okay that she wanted to take on such a big run. Not yet.

'The only way to improve is to test yourself,' Alex said, still annoyingly smug. 'And this looks far worse than it is. Really it's just a teeny step up from a blue.'

'Stop throwing colours at me. It's not helping.' The truth was she had barely slept again. An early start and an entire day of concentrating on a new sport had pushed her somewhere beyond tiredness to exhaustion. Muscles she hadn't even known she possessed ached, her feet hurt and all she wanted was a long, hot bath.

But she wouldn't be able to relax even once back in the room. Because Alex would be there. Their conversation from last night had buzzed around and around and around in her head until she wanted to scream with frustration. It had told her so much—and yet it had told her nothing at all. Why did he think he was broken?

'Look, I'll take it from here,' Alex told her instructor. 'Why don't you get going and you can start again tomorrow? I promise to return her in one piece.'

The instructor regarded her inscrutably from behind his dark lenses. He was tall, tanned and had a lithe grace that at any other time she would have had some pleasure in appreciating but it had been absolutely wasted on her today—she had been far too tired to attempt to flirt back.

'Tomorrow morning,' he said finally. It didn't sound like a request. 'You will be begging to try a black slope by the end of the week.'

'Never,' but she muttered it under her breath, just holding up a hand in farewell as he launched himself down, as graceful as a swallow in flight.

'So, you know another way down?'

Alex shook his head. 'It's on your own two skis only. And we need to hurry up. It's getting late.'

Flora bit her lip. She shouldn't be such a wuss

but staring down that great expanse made her stomach fall away in fear. It was the same reaction she'd had when Alex took her abseiling. She and mountains were not a good mixture. From now on she would stick to flat surfaces only. Like beaches; she was good with beaches.

'Okay.' She inhaled but the action didn't soothe her at all, her stomach still twisting and turning. Did people really do this for fun?

'I'll be right next to you,' he said, his voice low and comforting. 'I'll talk you through every turn.'

'Right.'

She pulled her goggles back down. Alex was right. It was just after four p.m. and the sun was beginning to disappear, the sky a gorgeous deep red. The slopes had been getting quieter so gradually she had barely noticed, but now it was obvious as she looked around that they were almost alone. Ahead of her the last few skiers were taking off, leaving the darkening slopes, ready to enjoy the huge variety of après-ski activities Innsbruck had to offer.

'It's a shame I didn't know you were here earlier.' Alex adjusted his own goggles. 'A couple of the hotel lodges are on this shelf. I'd have liked to show them to you.'

'It is a shame you didn't because I am never coming back here again.'

But he just laughed. 'You wait, when you've done it twice you'll wonder what all the fuss was about and be begging me to let you try something harder. Okay, count of three. One…two… three.'

Flora gritted her teeth and pushed off as he said three. The slope had been completely deserted as Alex began his countdown but as he reached the last number a group of snowboarders appeared from the slope above. Impossibly fast, impossibly spread out and impossibly out of control. Flora saw them out of the corner of her eyes and panicked, losing control of her own skis almost immediately as they swarmed by her, one of them catching her pole with his stick and spinning her as he sped by. She shouted out in fear and grappled for her balance, falling heavily, her ankle twisting beneath her.

'Oi!' But by the time Alex had caught her and yelled out a warning they were gone, their whoops and yells dissipating on the breeze. 'Are you okay?'

'I think so.' But Flora couldn't quite stop the little shivers of fear as Alex pulled her up. 'I thought they were going to run me right over.'

'I'll be putting in a complaint as soon as we get back down.' He retrieved her ski and handed it to her. 'Here you go, you're fine. I hate to hurry you, Flora, but it's getting pretty late. I don't want to guide you down in the dark. That *would* send you over the edge.'

'I know…' How long would it take? Her instructor had said that it was a ten-minute run but if Alex was going to talk her through it surely that would add on a few crucial minutes. She looked anxiously at the sky; the red was already turning the purple of twilight. Did they have fifteen minutes?

She put the ski down and slid her foot into the

binding, wincing as a spasm of pain ran across her ankle. 'Ow!'

'What's wrong?'

'I must have twisted my ankle as I fell. It's not too bad. I should be able to walk it off...'

'But you can't ski on it.' His mouth tightened. 'Those damned idiots.'

'Can't we ask for help?'

'We could. But I hate to ask the rescue guys to come out in the dark for a twisted ankle—especially as we took so long to get started. We're going to look pretty silly.'

'But we can't stay here all night.' Or did he still think she was going to make it down while they could still see? Flora swallowed. She was not going to cry.

Alex grinned. 'Panic not. I have a solution. Remember I said the ski lodges were on this shelf? This kind of situation is exactly what they're for. They should be completely kitted out because I know Camilla is hoping that some guests will try them out. It's hard to get permission to build anything up here so they're pretty special. Warm, comfortable and there should be food.'

'You built them for guests who got stranded on the slopes?' Now she thought she really might cry. Salvation! If the lodge only had running hot water then she would never ever complain about anything ever again. Her ankle was beginning to throb in earnest now and, standing still, Flora was all too aware of the chill bite of the wind.

'Really they're for people who want privacy or to spend time with nature. But this is as valid a reason as any. They're about half a mile this way. Can you manage?'

Half a mile? Through the snow? But if it was a choice between that and skiing down then Flora guessed it wasn't much choice at all. She nodded as convincingly as she could. 'Let's do it'

By the time they reached the first cabin the sun had disappeared completely and the twilight was moving rapidly from a hazy lilac grey to the thicker velvety purple that heralded night. Luckily both Flora and Alex had phones with torch apps on, which provided some illumination against the encroaching dark.

'Here we go,' Alex said with more than a hint of relief as they approached the pine grove. 'Good to know my memory hasn't forsaken me.'

The Alpine shelf was much narrower than the wide, buzzing nursery slopes and empty apart from the ski-lift way station. There wasn't even a *gasthaus* to serve up beer, hot chocolate and snacks, which meant that once the ski lifts had stopped running the guests would have total privacy.

'We built them in a pine grove, which means they have the advantage of shade in the much hotter summer months,' Alex explained as he guided her along the path. 'There are two in this grove and two even higher up. It makes them easier to service in pairs. But we've spaced them apart so guests should get the illusion of being all alone. In a fully catered, all-whims-pandered-to way.'

'I like the idea of being pandered to,' Flora said as Alex led her into the trees and down a little path. 'Oh, it's like a fairy tale cottage, hidden amongst the trees like that! A kind of sci-fi fairy tale anyway.'

It was a futuristic design, more of a pod than a traditional lodge with a low curving roof, built to blend into the landscape. 'They're so well insulated,' Alex said as Flora stopped still, trying to take it in fully, 'that they're warm in winter and cool in summer—although there's a stove in there to make it cosier.'

'It's gorgeous.'

It was, however, a little eerie arriving as darkness fell. Flora felt like a trespasser as they stamped their way through the snow to the door, discreetly situated at the side. 'It's as if we are the only two people in the world,' Flora whispered, not waiting to break the absolute silence with the sound of her voice. 'Like there's been some kind of apocalypse and we're all that's standing between the world and the zombies. Or the aliens.'

Alex shone his torch onto the keypad and punched at the buttons. 'Which would you rather?'

'Which would I rather what?'

'Zombies or aliens?'

This was so like their teen conversations that for one moment Flora forgot the cold, the ache in her ankle, the awkwardness of the last few days and was transported back to the roof of her house, accessed reasonably safely—although not with parental permission—from her attic window. She and Alex had spent many a summer night up there, staring up at the stars, discussing the Big Questions. Would you rather be eaten by a tiger or a shark? What would you do if you had twenty-four hours left to live? Were invisible? Could travel anywhere in time?

'Depends on what the aliens want, I suppose,' she said as she watched Alex swing the keypad open and extricate a key.

'If everyone's wiped out it can't be anything good.'

'No, but they might be allergic to something like salt water so we could do a mass extermination. With zombies you have to destroy their brains. That's quite a long process. Unless there were other pockets of survivors around. You?'

'Aliens would be cool. I always think zombies must reek.' He pushed the door open. 'Welcome, my lady.'

The door led into a spacious cloakroom with a flagstone floor. Hooks and shelves awaited, ready to dry out ski clothes or hiking jackets. Flora sank onto the nearest bench with a moan of bliss as she worked her boot off her sore ankle. It was a little swollen but not as bad as she'd feared and when she poked it nervously it didn't hurt too badly. She put her bare foot on the floor and squeaked in surprise. 'It's warm!'

'Underfloor heating. No expense spared here—and it means everything should dry out for tomorrow.' Alex was stripping off without any sense of embarrassment, his padded trousers and jackets neatly hung up, his boots put onto the bench provided, his socks stretched out ready to dry.

Flora's mouth dried. He was still decent—just—in his tight-fitting, thermal trousers and a

T-shirt. But they fitted him so well it was almost more indecent than if he had been half naked, highlighting every muscle. Alex was so tall, so rangy he seemed deceptively slight when in a suit but the form-fitting material made it clear he was in perfect shape.

The last thing she wanted to do was parade around in leggings and her T-shirt, the wide straps of her sports bra visible beneath the neckline. But neither could she stay bundled up in her padded clothes any more. The pod was beautifully warm.

She reluctantly pulled down the zip and shrugged off her jacket. Alex had already taken her boots and socks and when he turned back she handed him the jacket as if it were fine, as if she were as comfortable as he seemed to be. But she couldn't help noticing how his eyes fastened onto the generous curve of her chest, made far more prominent by the light, tight material, or how they lingered there.

'I don't suppose there's anything I can change into?'

He looked away, a faint colour on the high cheekbones. 'As a matter of fact I think they are keeping some spare clothes here for guests. I'll… er…go and see.' He backed towards the door that led into the rest of the pod, opened it and backed out, looking anywhere but at her.

What had he been doing? Staring at Flora's chest like, well, as any red-blooded male would. She might and did bemoan her curves but they were pretty magnificent—and, showcased by the tight black stretchy material, had been even more magnificent than usual.

Or was it just that he was more aware of her than he usually was, than he allowed himself to be? Of the way her hair waved around her face, of the sweetness in her eyes, the humour in her mouth?

'Did you find anything yet? Oh, my goodness. Alex, this is sensational!' Flora appeared at the door and looked around the room, her mouth open in admiration. The main room *was* sensational. It was also pretty intimate. He had designed the pod for romance. To allow the guests complete privacy, to make them feel as if they were the only people in the world. The skylights were the only windows, allowing the occupants to look up and see the night sky as they slept, although summer guests could slide open the back wall and enjoy the outside from the wooden terrace attached to the back of the pod if they wished.

A small kitchen area curved around the front wall; just a hob, a microwave, and a sink, the large, well-stocked fridge was back in the drying room. On the opposite side a second door led into the bathroom and a wood-burning stove was cosily tucked into the corner, a love seat, rugs and cushions heaped before it. But the main focus of the pod was the huge bed. It dominated the room; covered in throws and fake furs, it was big enough to fit several people. Flora's eyes settled on the bed and she swallowed. 'Very discreet.'

'Let me just look for some clothes and I'll let the hotel know where we are. They'll need to organise a cleaning crew to come up tomorrow. I know that Camilla is making sure every couple gets a night up here. She's hoping these pods will be a big hit with honeymooners.'

'Yes.' Flora's gaze was still fixed on the bed. 'I'm sure they will be.'

Alex ducked out of the room and into the quiet of the bathroom. Not that it was much better, the huge oval bath, designed for two, taking up most of the central space and the walk-in shower dominating the wall opposite. What had he been thinking? If they had set off down the mountain straight away they could have got back okay. Now here they were. Together. In a place designed for seduction. It made their hotel suite seem positively chaste.

Normally they would have laughed about it—and goodness knew that bed was big enough for them both to sleep completely sprawled out and never touch.

But these weren't normal times.

The cupboards, built in around the sinks, held fluffy towels and, he was glad to see, a selection of warm clothes. He pulled out one of the hotel-branded tracksuits for himself and looked for something for Flora. There was another track-suit, an extra-large that would swamp her, or a couple of white silky robes. Grabbing one of the robes, he handed it to her as he walked back into the main room. 'Why don't you…? There's a bath or a shower. I'll just get the stove lit and see what's in the fridge.'

She took the robe with a self-conscious smile of thanks and walked into the bathroom. Alex tried, he really did try, but he couldn't help watch her walk out of the room. The sway of her hips, her deliciously curved backside perfectly displayed in the tight leggings.

He stood there and inhaled. *Get a grip, Fitzgerald,* he told himself.

Ten minutes later the hotel had been contacted, the stove lit and Alex had raided the fridge for supplies. It wasn't hugely promising—unless he was bent on seduction. The fridge held several bottles of champagne, some grapes and cheeses.

The freezer was stocked full of hotel-prepared meals ready to pop into the microwave: creamy risottos, rich beef casseroles, chicken in white wine sauce. All of it light and fragrant. He'd have given much for a decent curry or a couple of bloody steaks. Substantial, mates' food, full of carbs and chilli, beer and laughter.

'I'm all done if you want the bathroom...' Flora stood by the bathroom door, her eyes lowered self-consciously. She had washed her hair and it was still damp, already beginning to curl around her face. The robe was a little too big and she had tucked it securely around her and belted it tightly. But no matter how she swathed herself in it, no matter how she tied it, she couldn't hide how the silky material clung to her curves, how the ivory set off the dark of her hair, the cream of her skin, the deep red of her mouth. She looked like a bride on her wedding night. Purity and decadence wrapped in one enticing package.

'If I want...' he echoed. His pulse was racing, the beat so loud it echoed through the room.

Twice in the last twenty-four hours he had walked away. Twice he had done the right thing.

He didn't think he could manage it a third time because when it came down to it he was only a man, only flesh and blood, and she was goddess incarnate.

He couldn't move. All he could do was stand and stare. She took a faltering step and then stopped, raising her eyes to meet his. 'Alex?'

'I want *you*.' There it was said. Words he had first thought at sixteen. Words he had never allowed himself to say, words he had made himself bury and forget. 'I want you, Flora.'

Her mouth parted and he couldn't take his eyes off it. Couldn't stop thinking about how it had felt under his, how she had tasted, how they fitted so perfectly he could have kissed her for ever.

'If I say yes...' Her voice was low, a slight tremble in it betraying her nerves. 'If I agree will you back out again? Because I'm not sure I can take another rejection, Alex.'

'I can't make you any promises beyond tonight,' he warned her. Warned himself.

She raised her eyebrows. 'I'm not asking for an eternity ring.'

'This will change everything.'

She nodded slowly. 'I think everything has already changed. We opened Pandora's box and now it's out there.'

He held her gaze. 'What is?'

'Knowledge.'

That was it. That was it exactly. Because now he knew. Knew how she felt, how she tasted, how she kissed, how her hands felt when they slid with intent. He knew the beginning; he had no idea how it ended. And oh, how he wanted to know.

And now that they had started they couldn't just pretend. Maybe this was what they needed, one night. One night to really know each other in every way possible. What was it Flora had said just two nights ago? That they should have done this in their teenage years?

He begged to disagree. He knew a lot more

now than he did then. No less eager, a lot more patient.

She still hadn't moved although her hands were twisting nervously and her eyelashes fluttered shut under the intensity of his gaze, shielding her expressive eyes as he watched her. 'You're so beautiful, Flora.'

Her eyes opened again, wide with surprise. 'Me? No, I'm too…' She gestured wildly. 'I'm too everything.'

'No, you're perfect.' He took a step nearer, his eyes trained on her, the small room narrowing until he could see nothing else, just damp, dark curls, ivory silk and long lashes over velvet dark eyes. Another step and another until he was standing right there. Within touching distance. 'Like a snow princess, hair as black as night…' He twisted a silky curl around his finger and heard her gasp. Just a little. 'Skin as white as snow.' He brushed her cheek lightly. 'Lips as red as rubies.' His finger trailed down her cheek and along the wide curve of her mouth.

She stared at him for one second more, her

breath coming quick, fast and shallow, and he could hold back no longer. He held her gaze deliberately as his hands moved caressingly down her shoulders, her arms until he reached her waist. He held them there for one moment, the heat of her flesh burning through the cool silk and then, in one quick gesture, he pulled at the knot holding her robe together. The belt fell away and as it did so the delicate ivory silk slithered back off first one white shoulder and then the other.

Flora reached out automatically to pull it back and he put out a hand to stop her.

'No, let it go.'

Her face flushed a fierce rose but she stood still in response to his words and allowed the robe to fall away, allowed herself to be unveiled to the heat of his gaze. She stood like the goddess she was named for, fresh as the spring.

Alex sucked in a breath, his stomach, his chest tightening as he saw her, really saw her. She was all softness and curves, all hidden dips and valleys, ready for an explorer's touch. He reached out reverently, to follow the curve of one breast. 'Let me worship you, Flora.'

She nodded. Just the once but it was all he needed as he took her hand and led her over to the bed. They had all night. He hoped it would be enough.

CHAPTER SEVEN

'I AM ABSOLUTELY STARVING.' Flora sat up, wrapping the sheet around her breasts as she did so. How could Alex parade around stark naked so unconsciously? It must be that public-school upbringing.

Not that she was complaining. Her eyes travelled across his finely sculpted shoulders, down the firm chest, the flat stomach and, as he turned, dwelled appreciatively on a pair of buttocks Michelangelo would have been proud to carve. No, she wasn't complaining at all.

'It's all that exercise,' he said as he disappeared through the cloakroom door, reappearing with a bottle of champagne, so chilled she could see the frost beginning to melt on the bottle.

'Mmm, the skiing was hard work,' she replied as demurely as she could and laughed at the affronted look he gave her.

'Minx,' he muttered. 'It'll serve you right if I let you go hungry.'

'Did I say skiing? Slip of the tongue. Oh, thank you…' She took the glass handed her and sipped it appreciatively. 'This is delicious.'

Don't be too happy, she warned herself. *Don't be too comfortable. This isn't real.* But it was hard not to be. It just felt so…so right. She should be embarrassed. This was Alex. Her oldest and bestest friend. They had just done things that definitely went against any friendship code but it wasn't awkward. It was horribly perfect.

He touched her as if he knew her intimately, as if he knew instinctively just what she wanted, what she needed, and she had wanted to touch every inch of him, nibble her way across every square inch of skin. No inhibitions—just want and need and giving and taking and gasping and moaning until she hadn't known where he stopped and she started.

Flora took another hurried sip of the champagne as her body tingled with remembered pleasure.

And now she could sit there, her hair tumbling down, her lips swollen and tender, muscles aching in ways that she was pretty sure had nothing to do with her earlier exertions on the slopes, clad only in a sheet and, although she might not feel confident enough to wander around in the buff, she was comfortable. Usually she jumped straight back into her clothes after lovemaking but with Alex she didn't feel too tall or too curvy. He'd made her feel fragile, desirable.

'Look how tiny your waist is,' he'd breathed as his hands had roamed knowledgeably across her body. 'Perfect,' he'd whispered as he'd kissed his way down her stomach. And that was how she'd felt. Perfect.

He sat down on the edge of the bed with that lithe casual grace she envied so much. 'I could heat up one of the frozen meals or, if you don't want to wait, there's cheese, biscuits and grapes?'

'Oh, cheese, please. That sounds perfect. Are you sure you don't want me to help?'

His eyes flashed with wicked intent. 'Nope, I don't want you to get out of that bed. Ever.'

'Sounds good to me.' How she wished this could *be* for ever, this perfect moment. The fire blazing in the stove, the stars bright in the sky-lights, she blissfully sated, lying in bed sipping champagne watching her man prepare dinner.

But he wasn't her man. And she needed to re-member that.

'Alex, are you awake?' They had dozed off some time after midnight, blissed out after an evening of champagne and lovemaking. Flora had no idea what time it was now; the cabin was com-pletely dark except for a faint reddish-gold glow from the stove.

Alex rolled over, throwing his arm across her as he did so, and she lay there, enjoying his weight on her, the skin against skin, the smell of him. 'Mmm?'

'Nothing,' she said. 'Go back to sleep.'

'Are you okay?'

'Yes, more than okay.' But she wasn't. The re-ality of what they had done was bearing down upon her. 'Are we?'

'Are we what?'

'Okay?'

He moved, propping himself up on one arm so that he could look down at her, a dark shadow in the dim room. 'Second thoughts, Flora?'

'No. I mean, it's a little late for that.'

He smoothed her hair back from her face, a tender gesture that made her chest ache and her eyes swell. 'Good. I don't know what tomorrow will bring, but right now I don't want to change a thing. Except wonder why we didn't do this a long time ago.' His hand trailed a long, languorous line down her face, down her throat, down and down. It would be so easy to let it continue its slow tortuous journey.

But his words reminded her of her vow. Her vow to try and help him. To make things right, somehow. She caught his wrist as it moved to her ribcage and held it. 'What happened, Alex?'

He laughed low and soft. 'Do you need me to explain it to you?'

She couldn't help smiling in response but she

clasped his wrist, her fingers stroking the tender skin on the inside. 'Not tonight. Then.'

He froze. 'Don't, Flora.'

But she knew. If she didn't ask him now he would never tell her. After all he had kept his secrets through the long, boozy university years, through long walks and bonfire heart-to-hearts. Through backpacking and narrow boats and noisy festivals. But tonight was different. To-night there were no rules.

'You came home from school,' she remembered. 'I had finished my GCSEs and you had done your AS Levels. I thought we would have another long summer together. But you were different. Quieter, more intense. More buttoned up. I had the most ginormous crush on you, which I tried to hide, of course. But that summer there were times when you looked at me as if...' Her voice trailed off.

'As if I felt the same way?' he said softly.

'We would be somewhere, just the two of us. On the roof talking, or lying on the grass, and I would look at you and it was as if time would stop.' Their eyes would meet, her stomach would tighten in delicious anticipation and she would find it hard to get her breath. 'And then nothing…' She sighed. 'I tried to kiss *you* that time. When we were watching that ridiculous horror film where all the teenagers died. I thought you would kiss me back but you didn't. You looked so revolted…' Her voice trailed away as she relived the utter humiliation, the heartbreak all over again.

He pulled his hand away from her gentle grasp, pushing the hair out of his eyes. 'Sometimes I wonder what would have happened if we had got together then. Do you think we'd be the friends we are now, our past relationship something to look back on nostalgically? Or maybe we would have ended badly and not speak at all. Or maybe we would have made it. Do you think that likely? How many people get together in their teens and make it all the way through college and university?'

'Not many,' she conceded. But *they* might have. If he'd wanted it.

'You changed that year.' He was still propped up on one arm, still looking down at her. She could smell the champagne on his breath, feel each rustle as he moved. 'Boys watched you all the time—and I watched them watching you. But you didn't even notice. I nearly made a move that New Year but I was away at school and we both had exams. So I told myself to wait. Wait till the summer.'

'What changed?' She hadn't imagined it; he had felt it too.

'My dad blamed me for my mother's death.' He said it so matter-of-factly that she could only lie there, blinking at the sudden change in conversation. 'Did I ever tell you that?'

'No.' She moved away, just far enough to allow her to sit up, hugging her knees to her chest as she tried to make out his expression in the dim light from the fire. 'I don't understand. How? I mean, it was suicide, wasn't it? Awful and tragic but nobody's fault.'

'He didn't want children. All he wanted was her, just her. You know my father. He's not the caring, sharing type. But she wanted a baby so much he gave in. He said it was the biggest mistake he ever made. That I was the biggest mistake… He was never really explicit but I think she suffered from fairly severe postnatal depression.'

A stab of sorrow ran her straight through as she pictured the lonely motherless little boy alone with an indifferent father. Allowed to grow up believing he was the cause of his mother's death. 'Oh, Alex. I'm so sorry.'

He shifted, sitting up beside her on the bed, leaning back against the pillows. 'She hid it from him, from the doctors, from everyone. Until I was two. Then she just gave up. She left a note, saying what a terrible mother she was. That she couldn't love me the way she was supposed to. That I would be better off without her…'

Flora touched his face. 'That doesn't make it your fault. You know that, right?'

'My father thought so.' His voice was bleak. 'That's when he began to work all hours, leaving me with a series of nannies, packing me off to boarding school as soon as he could. He told me it was a shame he had to wait until I was eight, that he would have sent me at five if he could have.'

Flora hadn't thought it was possible to think any worse of Alex's father. She had been spectacularly wrong. 'He's a vicious, nasty man. No wonder you came to live with us.'

He carried on as if she hadn't interrupted. 'He married again. I didn't really see much of him then, or of that particular stepmother, but apparently she wanted kids, wanted me around more and so the marriage broke up. He blamed me for that as well. I guess it was easier than blaming himself. And then that year, when I was seventeen, he remarried again.'

'Christa.' Oh, Flora remembered Alex's second stepmother with her habit of flirting with every male within a five-mile radius. She had made Flora, already self-conscious, feel so gauche, so huge like an oversized giant. 'Horry had a real crush on her. Do you remember how she used to parade around in those teeny bikinis when we came over to swim?' She laughed but he didn't join in and her laughter trailed off awkwardly.

'It was so nice at first to have someone care. Someone to bring me drinks, and praise me and take notice, as if I were part of a real family. It didn't even occur to me that other people's mums didn't ask their teenaged sons to rub suntan oil onto their bare back or sunbathe topless in front of them.'

Flora's stomach churned and she pressed her hand to her mouth. 'Alex...'

'She started to drop by my room for a chat when I was in bed. She'd stroke my hair and rub my shoulders.' His voice cracked. 'I was this big hormonal wreck. This woman, this beautiful, desirable woman, was touching me and I wanted her. I wanted her to keep touching me. But at the same time she revolted me, she was married to my *father*. And there was you...'

'Me?' Flora didn't know at which point her eyes had filled with tears, hadn't felt them roll down her face, it wasn't until her voice broke on a sob that she realised she was crying. Crying for the little boy abandoned by his father, for the boy on the brink of adulthood betrayed by those he trusted to look after him.

'I was falling in love with you that summer. But how could I touch you when at night…when I didn't turn her away…when I lay there waiting and didn't say no.'

'You were a child!'

'I was seventeen,' he corrected her. 'I knew what I was doing. I knew it was wrong—on every level. But I didn't stop her. I let her in my room, I let her into my bed and in the end I didn't just lie there…'

Flora swallowed, clutching her stomach, nausea rolling through her. That woman with her tinkling laugh and soft voice and Alex? And yet it all made a hideous kind of sense. How withdrawn he had become, the way he would look at her as if something was tearing him apart but Flora couldn't reach him. The knowing smile Christa would wear, the possessive way she'd clasp his shoulders. How had she been so blind?

She made an effort to sound calm, to let him

finally relieve himself of the burden he'd been carrying. 'What happened next?'

'By the end of the summer she had stopped being cautious. I didn't want… It was one thing at night, with the lights out—that was more like a dream, you know? As if it wasn't real. I would be back at school soon and the whole thing would just disappear. But Christa didn't want that. She started to try and kiss me in the house, run her hand over my shoulder in front of people. She wanted to make love in the pool, in the kitchen. The more I tried to pull away, the more determined she became. I was just a pet, her toy. She didn't want me to have any say in where or when or what. She was in control. And she was out of control. It was inevitable, I guess, that we'd be found out. My dad came home early one day and caught us.'

'He blamed you.' It wasn't a question. She'd seen the aftermath. Alex, white-faced, all his worldly possessions in one bag, determined to make his own way in the world.

'He told me I tainted everything I touched.'

'That's not true,' but he was shaking his head even as she protested.

'My mother died because she couldn't love me. My father hates me. My stepmother…there's something rotten at the heart of me, Flora.'

'No. No, there isn't.' She was on her knees and holding onto him. 'I love you, my parents adore you, for goodness' sake even Minerva loves you, in her own way. There *is* a darkness in your family but it's not you. It was never you.'

But she wasn't getting through; his voice was bleak, his face as blank as if it were carved out of marble. 'I saw you look at me, back then, so hopeful. As if you were expecting something more. But I had nothing to give. Christa took it all, like some succubus, taking another piece of my soul every time we had sex. All those girls at the ice rink, and the girls I date now. I felt nothing. I am incapable of feeling anything real. That's why I warned you to steer clear of me, Flora. There's nothing real inside me.'

She kissed him, his eyes, his cheeks, the strong line of his jaw, tasting the salt of her tears mingled with the salt on his skin. 'You are real,' she whispered as she pressed her mouth to his cold lips. 'I know you are.'

He didn't respond for a long moment and then, with an anguished cry, he kissed her back; hard, feverish kisses as if he were drowning and she the air. Flora held on and let him hold on in return. She didn't know who was saving who. And she wasn't sure that it mattered.

Alex knew the exact moment Flora woke up. She didn't move, didn't speak, but he knew. He had kept watch over her through the night. A lone knight guarding his lady. Her breathing, so slow and steady, quickened. Her body tensed. Was she wondering what would happen in the harsh light of day? What reality would mean after the passions, the confidences, the outpourings of the night before.

He wondered that too. He knew what had to be done but how he wished things were different. That he were different. 'Lukewarm left-over champagne or coffee?'

'Hmm?' She sat up unsteadily, brushing the long tangled curls from her face and scrubbing her eyes like a small girl, her eyes widening as she looked at him. Was she surprised that he was out of bed? That he was already dressed in jogging bottoms and his own top, showered, shaved and ready to go. 'You're not serious about the champagne?'

'It seems a shame to throw it away,' he teased, deliberately keeping his tone light. 'No. If it was chilled then that would be a whole different matter. There's eggs. We could make breakfast or would you rather have some back at the hotel? There's time. I texted your instructor to arrange a later meeting time.'

'A later time?' She sank back down onto her pillows dramatically. 'I was planning to spend all day in the spa today. I have barely slept...' She stopped, her cheeks pinkening in an interesting way. He wondered just how far down her blush crept—and then pulled his mind resolutely back to the matter at hand.

'Don't forget you have to get down the mountain first,' Alex said helpfully and was rewarded with a glare.

'Can't we just stay here for ever?' There was a plaintive note in her voice. He knew with utter certainty that it wasn't just the skiing she was thinking about. It was the aftermath. Of course she was.

His chest squeezed in sudden longing. *Stay here for ever.* Just Flora and Alex and a large bed and a supply of champagne. No facing the real world, no dealing with any situation. He inhaled long and deep, pushing the enticing vision away. 'What would we do when the food ran out? Hunt squirrels and roast them on the stove?'

'Not much meat on a squirrel.'

'Then we'd better return to real life. Sorry, Flora.'

She put out her hand. Part of him wanted to pretend he hadn't seen it, the other part was drawn to her, could no more walk away than he could stop breathing. He paced himself as he walked towards the bed, slow, unhurried steps, seating himself on the edge, deliberately not touching her.

'So, we pretend this hasn't happened.' She made it sound like a statement but he knew she needed an answer. Was she hoping he'd change his mind?

'That's best, isn't it? No need to complicate things further.' All he had to do was reach across, across just a few centimetres of rumpled white sheet. But it might as well have been metres, miles, oceans. Would she see a casual touch as encouragement? As a declaration?

Would he mean it as such?

He couldn't. He mustn't. If he allowed the slight torch she had always carried for him to blaze into brightness then all would be lost. He didn't know which would be worse—if it flickered and died when she discovered how hollow he really was for herself. Or if it continued to flame until he did something stupid, something unconscionable and broke her heart.

And he would.

His father's voice echoed through his mind.

Mocking him. *You taint everything you touch. Nobody could care for you. You disgust me.*

He couldn't cope if he lost Flora.

She touched his arm, a small caress. 'What are you thinking?' Ah, the million-dollar question and one he had always hated. He never got the answer right.

But he was compelled to tell the truth. 'I don't want you to hate me.'

She rounded on him, eyes blazing. 'I could never hate you. Why? Because of last night? You were very clear it was a one-night deal and I understood that. Don't make this into some kind of melodrama. It was just sex.'

But her eyes fluttered as she said the words and she couldn't look him in the eye.

'Good sex,' she amended. 'But, you know, I'm not planning to join a nunnery because there won't be a repeat.'

Alex didn't feel quite as comforted by her words as he should have done. This was the result he wanted, wasn't it? There was a little part of him that had always wondered *what if* about

Flora Buckingham and, sure, he had pointed out last night that a teen grand affair was bound to crash and burn, but still. He had wondered.

Now he knew. And even better she had no expectations beyond a cup of coffee and that he guide her safely to the bottom of the ski slope. By the time they got back to her parents' they would be their old selves. Only better. No more moments when he would look up and see a hopeful yearning in her face, no more watching her covertly as she walked across a room.

They had scratched that itch and it was satisfied. Let Flora move on to someone who deserved her. As for him? Well, maybe he would date a little less widely, date a little more wisely.

The thought made his chest feel as hollow as his heart.

Flora scrambled to her knees, the sheet held high against her chest, a thin barrier of cotton yet as effective as a cast-iron chastity belt. *You have no rights here.* 'We just need to get through the rest of this week. What do you want to do, tell Camilla that we quarrelled and get your room back? I mean…' as he raised an eyebrow at her '…you don't want to spend the next three nights on that sofa, do you? Unless…'

'Unless?' His pulse began to pound at the spark in her eye.

'We *are* meant to be dating, after all.'

'Flora…'

'Same rules,' she said hurriedly. 'No expectations, no protestations. What happens in Innsbruck stays in Innsbruck but, seriously. You can't stay on the sofa. We don't want to make Camilla suspicious. As long as we're both clear about the rules, what's the harm?'

'We get back on Christmas Eve,' he reminded her. 'Straight to your parents'. Won't they guess?'

'How? We promised not to let anything change our friendship and it'll be finished by then. Finished the moment we get into the taxi to drive to the airport. Maybe you were right, we would have had a mad teen thing, all drama and lust, and it would have been glorious—and it might have ruined us for ever. But we're older now, we're far more sensible. It doesn't have to ruin anything. But I reckon we're owed just a few days of crazy fun. We owe it to our younger selves.'

It was a convincing argument—if he didn't examine it too closely. 'I suppose we do at some point. Guess it's either now or when we're in the nursing home.'

'We might be married to other people when we're in the nursing home,' she pointed out. 'Plus right now I'm still reasonably pert and have all my own teeth. You might not be so keen when we're finally retired.'

His mouth dried. Did she know what she was offering? The rest of the week as a no-strings, full-fun affair. He didn't deserve it; he didn't deserve her. But he wasn't strong enough to turn her down.

You've always been weak. He thrust the insidious thought aside. They were supposed to be dating, they were sharing a room and they had just spent the night very much together.

'May as well be hung for a sheep as a lamb.' Her mouth curved into an irresistible smile.

'You do say the most romantic things. I can see why the girls love you. What's the very latest we have to be out of here?'

'We have about an hour if you want to eat, shower and change before your hot date with your dashing instructor. Why?'

'Well...' she let the sheet fall, just a little, not nearly enough '...I thought we might seal our deal with a kiss.'

CHAPTER EIGHT

'CAMILLA SEEMED IMPRESSED with your ideas.'

Flora put her hairbrush down and turned to look at Alex, admiring the lithe grace as he sprawled on the bed, completely at his ease as he looked through her sketchbook. 'It was like being summoned for an audience with the queen,' she said, her palms damp at just the memory. 'It's a good thing she can't actually raise those eyebrows of hers, she made me feel about six as it was.'

'That's just her way. I don't think she meant to question you quite so closely—she knew you would have no real idea of cost at this stage. We're still at the initial concepts.'

'How can I even think about putting costs in when she hasn't even decided which of your ideas she wants? Plus I have no idea of what I can actually source there—or what her actual budget is.' At least when she had worked in-house she hadn't had to worry about any of this part. She had been given a task, she'd completed it, easy—even if it had been dull and monotonous and about as creative as granola.

He turned another page, nodding as he looked at her carefully drawn plans. 'Relax. No one expects you to know any of this yet. Once Camilla gives us the go-ahead we can do a reconnaissance trip out there. We'll need to talk about money as well. The interior design is all subcontracted through my firm. Lola charged for each project as a whole but I could take you on as a contracted member of staff if that makes things easier.'

Flora froze. It would make things a *lot* easier. She had no idea about how much to charge if she freelanced, nor how often she could invoice, when she would get paid—or how she'd live until she did. But working with Alex? Travelling to Bali with him? It wasn't going to be the kind of cold turkey she thought she might need…

Because four nights in and she was already getting a little addicted to his touch. To the way his eyes seemed to caress her. To the way his hands most definitely did. To his mouth and the long, lean lines of his body.

She was in way over her head, barely graduated off the nursery slopes and yet heading full tilt down a black run and she didn't even care. 'Do we have to go on this evening's jaunt?' She allowed her eyes to travel suggestively over his body. 'I've seen the Christmas markets.'

'Not at night, you haven't, and yes, you do. Three-line whip. But we don't have to hang around in the bar after we get back if you would rather get some rest.' He smiled like the big bad wolf eyeing up Red Riding Hood.

'I do need a lot of rest,' she agreed solemnly. 'All this mountain air is exhausting me. I may also need a really long hot bath.'

'I was thinking about a bath too,' he said softly and she shivered at the intent look in his eyes as he slowly glanced from the large tub to her. 'I do feel particularly dirty this evening.'

A jolt of pure lust shot through her and Flora gripped the top of the dressing table, her knuckles white. What was she doing? How on earth could they ever return to their old, easy camaraderie after this? How would she manage when his hand was no longer hers to hold, when she couldn't run her fingers over the soft skin on the inside of his wrists, when she couldn't kiss her way along the planes of his face and down his neck?

She had dreamt of this for so long that it all felt completely right, completely fitting. Stepping back again? That was going to hurt. But she had promised him that it would all be fine, that she would be fine, they would be fine and she couldn't let him down. She would just have to keep smiling and pretend her heart wasn't shattering into millions of little pieces.

'Okay.' She turned back to the mirror and outlined her mouth with the deep red lipstick. She'd almost got used to the striking colour over the last few days. It sent out a statement of confidence that she might not feel but that she could fake. She caught up a silk scarf, a midnight blue patterned with abstract snowflakes, and knotted it around her neck, the accessory adding some much-needed style to the cream jumper and blue velvet skinny jeans she'd chosen for their warmth. 'I'm ready.'

Alex caught her hand as they left the hotel room, an easy gesture. She fought to keep her hand loosely clasped in his, not to curl her fingers tightly around and hold on, never letting him go.

'You can help me choose Christmas presents,' he said as they made their way along the wide corridor to the stairs. 'I haven't managed to buy any yet. I expect yours were all done and dusted by September.'

'This year's fabric was designed and printed by then,' she agreed. Twice a year Flora got several of her designs printed up into silks and cottons, which she then used to make the cushions and scarves she sold online. She also combined her own designs with vintage fabrics to create quilts, which she made to order. 'I've made both

Mum and Minerva clutch bags. I hope they like them. I don't think Minerva has ever worn last year's skirt.'

'Strawberries and cream isn't particularly Minerva,' he pointed out. 'But it was a beautiful design. I'm sure she really appreciates it. Apron for your dad?'

'Of course.' Every year she made her father a new apron and a selection of tea towels and he always made sure they were prominently displayed in every tutorial and photoshoot. 'I've bought dolls for the twins and made them entire wardrobes.' She had also made shirts for Horry, Greg her brother-in-law and Alex in the same pattern as the scarf she was wearing this evening. Flora always made her presents; she suspected Minerva at least would rather she stuck to scented candles and bath salts but Flora loved to create things, especially for the people she cared about.

'As we're in Austria I'm thinking glass all round, animals for the littlies, crystal glasses and bowls for the adults. Too obvious?'

'No, they'll love them. It's unfair how you always manage to pull the perfect present out of the bag last minute when some of us plan all year round.' She squeezed his hand in mock protest and he grinned.

'Not unfair, it's because I have good taste.'

And money to spare, she wanted to retort—but she didn't. After all, he'd always managed to find the right thing, even when he was at college and working three jobs in order to pay his way, refusing to allow the Buckinghams to house and feed him rent free. This man who didn't think he was worth loving.

'I was thinking,' she said hesitantly. They hadn't discussed anything personal since the night at the ski lodge, a tacit agreement to keep the week as carefree as they could.

'Careful…'

She elbowed him. 'Ha-ha. Don't you have any grandparents? Uncles, aunts?'

'Trying to get rid of me, Flora?'

'Never. It just seems odd, that's all. There must be someone.'

But he was shaking his head. 'As far as I know my father's parents died before I was born and he was an only child—not that he'd tell me if there were a hundred relatives out there, I suppose. As for my mother, I did see my grandmother when I was much younger but she gave up. Either my father frightened her off or I...'

Flora squeezed his hand. 'Don't even go there with the "or I". If she disappeared I would bet all my Christmas presents your father was behind it. You should try and track her down. She might have some answers.'

'Maybe.' But he didn't sound convinced and she didn't want to push any further.

Flora was surprised by how at ease she felt as they approached the hotel lounge. It was busy; the guests buzzing as they discussed their impending visit to Innsbruck's famous Christmas markets, sampling the food and drink on offer and purchasing some last-minute gifts. Normally she'd find such a noisy and full room intimidating, hang behind Alex as he strode confidently in, let him be the one to mingle, she following where he led. But over the last couple of days she had struck up a few acquaintances and greeted her new friends with pleasure when Alex disappeared over to the other side of the room to charm an influential broadsheet journalist who was considering a magazine feature on Alex's work.

'I hear you skied down several red runs today,' Holly, the travel journalist Flora had met on the first evening, teased her. Flora was the only learner in the entire hotel and many people were watching her progress with encouragement and interest. 'We'll have you out on the blacks before we leave.'

'Not this trip.' Flora shook her head emphatically. 'But, I have to say—and I am amazed I am about to admit this—I think I'll come back and ski again. It has been sort of fun. Although I still prefer the hot-chocolate, hot-tub part of the proceedings most!'

'If I was sharing a hot tub with your boyfriend I think that would be my favourite part of the evening too.' Holly looked over at Alex, a wistful expression on her face. He was casually dressed: jeans, a dark green cashmere jumper, hair characteristically tousled. There were more obviously handsome men in the room, more famous men—richer men—but somehow he stood out.

Or maybe it was just that Flora instinctively knew where he was at every moment. Her north star.

Flora stood back to let one of the other women pass by. Although she recognised her they hadn't spoken during the week; the celebrity guests, mostly socialites and gossip-magazine staples, tended to keep to their own tanned, designer-clad selves and only a few people like Alex passed from one group to the other with no hint of unease. Bella Summers was gossip-magazine gold—an ex-model, TV presenter and extremely keen skier, she had been invited to bring the launch week a sprinkle of glamour and help create a buzz around the hotel.

'Oh, my goodness.' To Flora's amazement Bella stopped dead in front of her, staring at her neck in undisguised envy. 'Your scarf! Isn't that the same one Lexy Chapman is wearing in this week's *Desired*?' Her eyes flickered to Flora's face, curiosity mingling with undisguised surprise. 'Where on earth did you get it?'

'This scarf.' Flora touched it self-consciously. 'No, it can't be the same. It must be a coincidence.'

'It is exactly the same. That abstract snowflake print is unmistakeable,' Bella Summers insisted. 'Mitzy, come here. Isn't this the same scarf Lexy wore on her date with Aaron? The one in *Desired*?'

Another tall, skinny, elegant girl loped across to join them. The two of them stood there gazing at Flora's neck like a couple of fashion-hungry vampires. 'Yes, that's the one,' she said. 'Hang on. I think I left the magazine on the shelves over there. It only came out yesterday. Luckily a shop in Innsbruck stocks it.'

It can't be the same. It's just a coincidence, Flora told herself. It was always happening, designers inspired by the same things coming up

with similar designs. Or of course work got pla-
giarised; small solo outfits like hers were particularly vulnerable.

Unfortunately it was a much more likely scenario than the other—It girls and style icons just
didn't buy from small solo nobodies like her. She
didn't even have a brand name or a website of
her own, using an Internet marketplace to sell
the handful of items she produced each year.

'Yes, I knew it.' Mitzy and Bella came back
waving the latest copy of *Desired* triumphantly.
'Here you go. Flora, isn't it? Look.'

Flora took the glossy magazine from them.
Desired was an upmarket weekly combining
fashion, gossip and lifestyle in easily digest-
ible sound bites and pictures. It was already
open at the page they wanted, the street-style
section. Photos of fashion-forward celebrities
out and about, their outfits and accessories
critiqued. Girls like Lexy Chapman were staples on this page—as were girls like Bella and
Mitzy, although neither had the cool kudos of
Lexy Chapman.

Normal people didn't have a hope of appearing on the hallowed pages, no matter how stylishly they dressed. And Flora was too awkward for style.

But maybe, just maybe she had some influence after all.

She sucked in a deep breath as her eyes skimmed over the photo. Lexy Chapman was casually dressed for her date with her on-off rock-star boyfriend in tight-fitting skinny jeans and a cream, severely cut silk shirt visible underneath an oversized navy military coat. The starkness of the outfit was softened by the scarf, tied around her slender neck with a chicness Flora could only envy.

She skimmed the brief wording, her heart thumping.

How does she do it? Once again Lexy Chapman strips back this season's must-have styles to their bare essentials combining masculine tailoring with military chic.

A clever touch is the snowflake motif scarf, which adds a feminine twist and is a clever nod to the season.

The article was followed by a list of the clothes and accessories, with price, designer and website. Sure enough, right at the bottom…

Scarf, Flora B, £45

It was followed by her website address.

'Hang on.' Mitzy snatched the magazine back off Flora and read the article again. 'Flora B? Is that you? Oh, my goodness, you have to let me have one of your scarves. What other designs do you have? Do you have any on you?'

'I…' Flora tried to think. What did she have in stock and ready made up? 'Sure. When we get back from Innsbruck I'll show you my web shop. I only make up a couple of patterns a year so it does depend on what's left.'

'Exclusive.' Mitzy nodded in satisfaction. 'Good.'

'If you could just excuse me…' Flora tore her eyes away from the page, her head giddy. What if the photo had generated more interest? She hadn't checked her orders since she had arrived in Austria. It wasn't as if they usually came flooding in—more than three a week would be a rush—and she had designated the Friday of last week the last day she could guarantee Christmas delivery. 'I just need to check on something.'

Flora was glad to escape from the noisy room. The mood had changed as the news flew through the room. People—especially the celebrity clique—were looking at her differently, actually seeing her. Or seeing her value to them. One scarf in one picture. Was that all it took to go from zero to person of interest?

With this lot it appeared so.

She hurried upstairs, back to their recently vacated suite. It looked different, smelt different with Alex's belongings casually strewn around. His laptop was set up on the desk in the corner, a pair of his shoes left by the door. His book on the side table—not that he'd been doing much reading. Or work. Neither of them had. She liked it. Liked the casual mingling of their belongings.

Flora's phone was in a drawer along with her charger. She hadn't wanted it on, hadn't wanted to be in contact with the outside world, to be reminded that this short idyll was temporary. She switched it on, her mind whirling while it powered up. Would this mean a run on her small amount of stock? If so would it be worth investing in more fabric? How would she fund it? How could she make and store decent amounts of stock in her small rented room? What if she did invest and demand dried up?

She shook her head. Talk about counting chickens! She might find that Mitzy and Bella were the only people who had even noticed the scarf—and only because she was wearing it.

Her phone sprang into life, pinging with a notification—and another and another like a much less musical one-note version of the sleigh bells. Social-media notifications, emails, voicemails. Flora stared at her buzzing screen and felt her head spin. She had only started the social-media accounts for her business to stop her sister, Minerva, nagging her but rarely used them. She didn't know what to say to her tiny handful of followers.

'Flora?' The door had opened while she watched

the notifications multiply. 'We're heading off.' Alex paused, waiting for her to answer but she couldn't find the words. 'What is it?'

She handed him the phone and Alex stared at it incredulously.

'What? Have you just won a popularity contest?'

'I don't know. I think it's about a scarf but I don't know where to start.'

'A scarf? Is this the same scarf that has half the women downstairs frothing at the mouth?'

She nodded, the surrealism of the situation disorientating her. 'Either that or I've won the lottery, been photographed kissing a boyband member or I am a long-lost princess. There are over fifty voicemail messages and I don't know how many emails.'

The phone beeped again. 'More than fifty...' he peered at the phone '...although it looks as if at least half are from Minerva. Hold on.' He put the phone back down a little gingerly, as if it were an unexploded bomb. 'I am going to make our apologies to Camilla and I'll help you sort this out.'

'Your glass animals…'

'Can wait. I'll pop down tomorrow before the Christmas Ball. Wait here. Don't touch anything.'

Flora sank onto the sofa, almost too distracted to notice just how uncomfortable it was. Her phone beeped a few more times and then it was mercifully silent. She unlooped the scarf from around her neck and passed it from one hand to the other, the silk cool under her fingertips. A midnight-blue silk with her snowflake design on it. She had only printed one roll of fabric. It was destined for the central square and edging for a handful of quilts, as the cuff lining on the shirts she had made Alex, Greg and Horatio, the lining of a few bags, some cushions and twenty or thirty scarves.

Her fabric design and sewing were a hobby that barely paid for itself. It took up time she should be spending trying to get her talents noticed so she could work in-house again or at least pick up some freelance contracts in her own field and leave the world of temping far behind.

She didn't do it for money or fame. The truth was it just made her happy.

Just...

'Right.' Alex appeared back, the magazine in his hands and open at the fateful page. 'It looks like this *is* the cause of all the fuss. I've just been asked by at least ten people if I can get them one of these scarves and they are all prepared to pay a great deal more than forty-five pounds.' His brow wrinkled as he looked at the photo. 'Who is this woman?'

'You know who she is. That's Lexy Chapman.'

He looked blank. 'Nope. What does she do?'

That was a good question. What did she do apart from look cool and date famous people? 'Right now she's making my scarves sought after.'

He took the scarf from her loose grasp and held it up to the light, turning it this way and that. 'I didn't know you sold them. I just thought it was a hobby.'

'It is a hobby.' She turned away from his scrutiny, jumping to her feet and retrieving her phone from the side. 'I have a little online shop, to help fund my projects, that's all.'

'Is it?' But he didn't probe any further. 'Okay, this is how we're going to play it. You listen to your voicemails and make a note of all the names, messages and numbers and we'll see who you need to call back and when. I'll log onto your email and social-media accounts, put a holding message on them and see if there's anything really urgent. What do you think?'

Flora nodded. 'Thanks, Alex.' It was what she would have done but having some help would make it easier—and a lot faster. 'I really appreciate it.'

'Come on, what else are friends for?' But he didn't quite meet her eyes as he said it. Worry skittered along her skin, slow and sure as a cat on a fence. Had grabbing a few days' pleasure meant the end of everything? Like a gambler staking everything on one last spin and losing. Was the thrill of watching the wheel turn and the ball hover on first red and then black worth it? That moment when anything was possible worth the inevitable knowledge that nothing was?

He opened his laptop. 'I hope you can remember your passwords. Right, where shall I start?'

It didn't take too long for Flora to open up each of her accounts for Alex, averting her eyes from the dozens of messages and multitudes of new followers. She retreated to the bed with a notebook, a pen and her phone ready to start listening to her messages. Alex was right; Minerva had been calling consistently all day. Flora steeled herself and began to listen.

Minerva, a fashion buyer from Rafferty's, one of London's most exclusive department stores, a couple of magazines, Minerva, Minerva—Minerva again. By the time she got to her sister's seventh message Flora knew she'd better call her back.

'At last!' Her sister didn't bother with formalities like 'Hello' or 'How's Austria?'

'Evening, Merva,' Flora said pointedly. But the point, as always, was lost.

'I'm glad you've decided to emerge from hibernation. I couldn't get hold of you or Alex.'

'We've been working.' Minerva hadn't been able to get hold of Alex either? It was most unlike him not to have one phone in one hand and the other in front of him—although now Flora thought about it she had only seen him check his work phone and emails a few times—and she hadn't seen his personal phone at all. Not since the ski lodge. Maybe he was enjoying living off grid just as she was. She glanced over at him. He was tapping away, frowning with concentration. Her entire body ached at his nearness.

Minerva's tart tones recalled her to the matter at hand. 'Working? Whatever. So who is handling this for you? I've asked around but no one has admitted it. Not surprisingly, I would never let you disappear at such a crucial time in a campaign. Unless that's part of the plan, to drum up more interest? Too risky, I would have thought.'

Handling, campaign? It didn't take too long

for a conversation with her sister to feel like a particularly nasty crossword where the clues were in one language and the answers another. 'Minerva,' she said patiently. 'I have no idea what you're talking about.'

'Of course it didn't take too long for people to work out who you were, thanks to Dad's aprons. Another serious misstep. You really need him in the latest designs in this crucial period while you're establishing yourself, although I do think the whole apron thing is a bit saccharine myself. Still, it establishes you as part of that quirky routine he has going on. But you should be here, not drinking schnapps and frolicking on mountains.'

Flora froze. How did her sister know? 'I haven't been frolicking,' she said, hating how unconvincing she sounded. Alex looked up at her words and his mouth curved wickedly.

'I beg to differ,' he said, too quietly for Minerva to hear, and Flora's whole body began to simmer in response.

'Look,' she said hurriedly, wanting to get Minerva off the phone, everything else replied to and Alex back here, on the bed, while she was still allowed to want that. 'You are going to have to speak in words of one syllable. What are you talking about?'

Her sister huffed. 'Who is handling your PR for the Lexy Chapman campaign? I hope you know how humiliating it is for me that you didn't even ask me to pitch.'

Her what? 'Merva, there isn't a campaign.'

Disbelieving silence. 'You expect me to believe that the most stylish woman in Britain was photographed in your scarf by a complete coincidence?'

'I know you too well to expect anything, but yes. That's what happened. Goodness, Merva, as if I would ever not ask you in the highly unlikely event I was going to run a campaign. My inbox is full, my social media is insane, I have voicemails from scary influential people I don't dare call back and I'm terrified even thinking about logging onto my shop because I don't have enough stock to fulfil half a dozen orders.' She could hear her voice rising and took a deep breath. 'Come on, even I know enough not to launch a campaign like that.'

Minerva was silent for a moment and Flora could picture her as if they were in the same room, the gleam of excitement in her eyes, the satisfaction on her cat-like face. Her sister loved a challenge—and she always won. 'I need you,' she added.

'I know you do,' but Minerva's voice wasn't smug. She sounded businesslike. 'Leave everything to me. I'll take care of it all. Right. I need to know who has left you a message and why, all your social-media account details and you need to forward me every email. Oh, and let me know your current stock list. You won't be able to supply everyone so let's make sure you only focus on the people who matter. When are you back?'

'The day after tomorrow.' *Too soon.*

'Christmas Eve? The timing is really off. We'll lose all momentum over the holidays.'

'Yes, well, next time I inadvertently sell a scarf to a style icon I'll make sure she only wears it at a more convenient time.'

'Luckily…' it was as if she hadn't spoken '…I am a genius and I can fix this. Right, I want all that information in the next half-hour. Do not speak to a single journalist without my say-so, do not promise as much as a scrap of fabric to anyone—and, Flora? Keep your phone on.' Minerva rang off.

'Goodbye, Flora. It was nice speaking to you. The kids send their love,' Flora muttered as she put the phone down, her head spinning. 'Alex, it's okay. Minerva is going to save the world armed with a few Tweets and her contact list.'

'Thank goodness.' He pushed the chair back. 'There are some hysterical women out there—and some even more hysterical men who think they will never have sex again if they don't produce one of your scarves on Christmas morning. No pressure.'

She flopped back onto the bed, her phone clutched in her hand. 'I just need to get all this information to Minerva and then we can head into Innsbruck—if you still want to go, that is?'

'We could.' His voice was silky; that particular tone was the one that always made her blood heat up, her body ache. 'Or we could use our time far more productively.'

Flora propped herself up on one arm and looked at him from under her lashes. 'Productive sounds good. What do you have in mind?'

He picked up the scarf and twisted it into a slim rope, pulling it taut between his hands before looking back at her, a gleam in his eye. 'Such a versatile material. I'm sure we'll think of something.'

CHAPTER NINE

'HERE YOU ARE. I was beginning to think you'd got yourself stranded in a ski lodge again.' Alex allowed the hotel door to swing closed behind him and leaned against the wall, watching her appreciatively. 'Room in there for a little one?'

'It's not that sort of bath,' Flora told him, slipping a little further into the bubbles so that all he could see was her hair piled into a messy knot on the top of her head. Little tendrils had escaped and were curling in the heat; his hands itched with the need to touch them.

'What other sort is there?' It was hard to make conversation knowing that she was naked and wet. Totally exposed and yet completely veiled. Whose idea was it to put a bath in the middle of the bedroom? Probably Lola's. If he weren't so angry with his ex-designer's lack of profession-alism he would track her down and offer her a bonus. It was genius. That was it; every building he designed from now on would have a bath in the middle of a room. Even if it was supposed to be an office. Or a shopping centre.

Flora moved and the water lapped against the side of the bath, the sound another tantalising reminder of her undressed state. 'This is a ball-preparation bath. It involves all kinds of depilation, exfoliating, filing and moisturising.'

'Sounds serious.' He took a step closer to her, then another. Each step unveiled a little bit more, the tilt of her face, rosy from the hot water, her long neck a delicate blush pink. Then bubbles, clothing the rest of her, although if he craned his neck and looked really hard there were a few intriguing gaps in the white suds revealing hints of interesting things.

'It is. Deadly serious. Did you find everything you wanted at the Christmas markets?'

'Yep. Eventually. I had a long hard morning on the slopes first. Gustav was desolated that you missed your last day's lessons. He had a particularly challenging slope ready for you. So what have you been doing while I was skiing and shopping?'

'Ugh.' The sigh was long and heartfelt. 'I have spent most of the day sat at my laptop video-calling Minerva. Although you'll never guess what she was wearing…'

Alex's mouth curved into a slow smile. He knew Minerva. 'Last Christmas's skirt.'

'*And* a scarf I gave her a couple of years ago in her hair. Nice to know my presents suddenly have value. Not that I should complain. She has sorted everything. Although she's set up a couple of interviews for next week.' She sounded apprehensive. 'Face to face and photos, which is not good news after all the *Kaffee* and *Kuchen* I've had—especially the *Kuchen*.'

'Don't forget your dad's five-course Christmas dinner,' Alex reminded her helpfully and laughed as she groaned.

'Don't—you know how upset he gets if we skip anything—and he thinks that seconds is the only real way of gauging a dish's success. But I *am* really grateful. She's taken over the social media and created waiting lists, replied to all the emails and soothed every fashion editor's ruffled feathers. Her poor staff, two days before Christmas, and she pulled a three-line whip. I almost feel guilty that I'm luxuriating in this bath—and then I remember that this too is work.' She sank a little further into the steaming water with a small purr of pleasure.

'How much is she charging you?'

'That's the best bit. It's my Christmas present. She's keeping the exorbitantly expensive scented candles she *had* bought me, which are far more her bag anyway, and is giving me her staff's toil instead, nicely wrapped with a big bow on top.'

Alex bit back a smile. 'How very generous of her, although a cynical person would point out that it's not doing her any harm. You're the one in demand. She's handling the buzz, not creating it.'

'It's two days before Christmas and I'm about to go to a ball. No cynicism allowed.'

Alex perched on the edge of the bathtub and looked down at her. 'How are you feeling about your designs being out there?'

Her eyelashes fell. 'Half excited, half terrified. Naked—and not just because I am.'

'That's how it should be,' he told her. 'Even when you're working to a brief there should be a little something of you in there. You should be exposed, otherwise you haven't gone as far as you could have.'

She raised an eyebrow. 'Always? Even when I had to rebrand the Village Inns wine bar chain and they wanted pinks and lime greens and bits of fruit everywhere?'

'Especially then. Otherwise what's the point? That's why I struck out on my own so early. I wanted to be able to pick and choose my own work—that doesn't mean I don't listen to my clients though. There has to be a balance. I wonder...' He paused, not wanting to push too much when she was still adjusting.

'Wonder what?'

Oh, well, in for a penny... 'At your degree show it was obvious your passion—and a huge amount of your talent—lay in textile design. It shows every Christmas, with every gift you make. But you've never tried to make it your career. You set your sights on interior design and took the first job you were offered even though you hated their whole brand.'

'Hate's a bit strong...' she protested. 'Wholeheartedly disliked maybe. That's why it would never have worked with Finn. Even if he hadn't been a golf-obsessed workaholic, he really loved the branding.'

'It wouldn't have worked with Finn because he was an idiot.' Alex's teeth began to grind just at the thought of Flora's ex. How a girl with such good taste had such bad taste in men he would never know.

Not that he was any improvement. Actually that was untrue. A warthog was an improvement on Finn.

'Good point.'

'So why haven't you tried to sell your designs before? Into shops or to fashion designers? It seems like the perfect path for you.'

'I guess because I don't design fabric to make money. I do it because I love it.'

'Exactly. Why shouldn't you do what you love? I do. Your whole family does. Don't you deserve to as well?'

She slithered further down into the water, as if she were hiding from the question. 'It's different for you. You know what you want. You don't let anything stand in your way. That thing you said, about having a piece of you in everything you do? I see that in your work. In this hotel, in your designs for Bali. And it's wonderful. But it's so exposing.'

'And that frightens you?'

'If people hate the neon limes, and they mostly will, then that's fine. It's not *my* creatives they hate. I'm just following the brief. But if they hate my scarves or my quilts or my bags, things I've poured love and attention into? That feels like I've failed—again. Like I've been rejected again. I don't want the things I love tainted.'

Alex reached out and twisted one of the piled-up tendrils of dark silky hair around his finger. 'Everything worthwhile comes with a price, Flora.'

She sighed. 'Sometimes the price is too high. I don't want to feel that exposed. I've spent my whole life being judged. Noticed because of my height, leered at because I was a teenager with big boobs, every teacher pointing out how unlike my siblings I was. My parents dragging me onto TV. I just want to be anonymous.'

His voice softened as he pulled at the curl. 'But you're out there now. You need to harden up, think about the next step.'

'It's not that easy though, is it? I need money to expand—to buy fabric, a better machine, a studio, somewhere to keep stock. Even if I stay small and exclusive I don't think keeping my stock in boxes under my bed is going to cut it—or make me enough to live on!'

'That's where I have good news. Camilla caught me on the way in. She very much wants you to work on the next three hotels and is prepared to pay for the privilege. Do you trust me to negotiate you a good deal?'

Flora sat up, the water sloshing as she did so. It was so deep she was still respectably covered, just her shoulders rising from the white foam like Aphrodite. As enticing and tempting as Aphrodite. 'A good deal? Does she know that my previous experience pretty much consisted of that awful pink fruit décor and the teapot theme for those cosy retro cafés? And let's not forget the chintzy bedding range. This is a massive step up. I should be paying her!'

He grinned. 'All she's heard for the last twenty-four hours are her guests desperate to get hold of your work. If she can announce right now, while the buzz is still big, that you're the designer for her next three hotels then that's quite a coup for Lusso Hotels. I told you she likes to work with people who have a marketable story and right now that's you. It's a great way to get publicity for both here and for her future plans.'

She bit her lip. 'I suppose. And she was already considering me so nothing much has changed.'

'Nothing much but the price tag. If you sub-contract to me then I can pay you monthly— which will give you some stability while you step up your own designs as well. Like all projects there will be weeks when you don't need to do much for Lusso Hotels and other weeks when it will be frantic. But the subcontract could include studio space at my office for the length of the contract and if you use it for your other work then that's fine. It'll be yours.'

'That would be great. At least that's the space issue sorted.'

Alex had saved the best bit for last. 'And she would like to see a touch of your own style in your plans for the Bali hotel, so I guess I was wrong when I said to watch the whimsy.'

Her eyes sparkled. 'Really? You were wrong? Can I have that in writing?'

'Watch it.' He dipped a hand in the bath and scooped up a little bit of water.

'Don't you dare…this is a serious bath. I already told you.'

'Don't I dare what? Do this?' He trickled the water slowly onto the exposed part of her chest, his heartbeat quickening as he watched the silvery drops trace a trail down her skin until they disappeared into the deep vee between her breasts.

'Or this?' she countered sweetly and before he could move away she grabbed the front of his shirt and hauled him into the bath, laughing as he landed on top of her. 'Mind my hair. I don't want to get it wet!'

Alex raised himself onto his hands and knees. 'Now look what you've done. My clothes are all soaking.' He rocked back onto his heels, ignoring the splash of the water as it sloshed over the side of the bath. 'I'm going to have to take them off. You wanted a serious bath, Flora Buckingham? You've got one.'

Her eyes didn't leave his as he pulled the sopping-wet shirt over his head, or as he began to unbutton his trousers. 'Bring it on,' she said, her voice breaking huskily, belying the tough words. 'If you think you're man enough.'

'Oh, Flora,' he promised her as his trousers and boxers followed his shirt over the side of the bath. 'I'm more than man enough. Just wait and see.'

* * *

'Come on, what's taking so long?' Alex sounded impatient as he rapped on the bathroom door. Again.

Flora rolled her eyes at her reflection. 'It's not my fault I had to redo my hair,' she called back. 'I told you not to get it wet.'

He didn't answer for a moment, then: 'Regrets, Flora?'

'That my hair got wet? It might have been worth it.' That didn't mean she was entirely regret free but she wasn't going to admit that to him. Or to herself. Not tonight. It was their last night, they were going to a Christmas ball and she looked, even if she said so herself, pretty darn smoking.

The dress she had bought from the vintage shop in Innsbruck was deceptively demure. The chiffon cap sleeves revealed just a hint of her shoulder and the neckline hugged the tops of her breasts, the bodice narrowing at her waist before flaring out again, the full skirt finishing at her calves. She saw more revealing outfits every day in the offices she temped in.

Deceptively demure. It covered everything and yet…was it the bright red, a shocking contrast to the paleness of her skin? Was it the fit, the way it clung like a second skin? Or was it the way it defined and enhanced every curve so that, despite the modest neckline, Flora felt more exposed than if she was venturing out in just her bra?

Maybe it was because she was so obviously and evidently dolled up? Her hair tumbled free in carefully arranged curls, her lips were red and her eyes outlined in dark, dark kohl and, for once, she had slipped her feet into heels, which would make her taller than most of the men in the room.

But Alex would still top her.

'Flora…'

'Okay, okay, I'm coming.' She took one last look. Yes, she was definitely smoking—either that or she looked like a pin-up version of Mrs Claus but either way she had no choice. She had nothing else even remotely suitable for a Christmas ball. Inhaling deeply, Flora opened the bathroom door.

And stared. It was so unfair. Here she was. Two hours later. Hair washed, curled, sprayed and teased. Body plucked free of each and every stray hair, moisturised and buffed, face artfully painted, nails filed and polished, dress squeezed into, shoes forced on. And what had Alex done? Showered, shaved and shrugged himself into his tux.

She swallowed, her mouth dry. The stark black, relieved only by the crisp white of his shirt, suited him, brought out the auburn glints in his hair, made his eyes greener than grey. He looked like a stranger; a powerful, imposing and hot stranger.

A powerful, imposing and hot stranger who was staring straight back at her, mouth slightly open and a dazed expression on his face.

'Will I do?'

He didn't answer straight away, just nodded.

'Yes,' he said, clearing his throat. 'You look incredible.'

Heat flooded her cheeks at the expression in his eyes. 'Fine feathers,' she said a little unsteadily. 'Put anyone into a dress like this and they'll scrub up okay.'

'No.' His eyes were so intent, heat smouldering in their depths, that she felt completely exposed, naked. 'The dress is…' His gaze travelled over her, burning a trail onto her, marking her, claiming her. 'The dress is sensational. But it's all you, Flora. You'd look just as amazing in a sheet.'

'Thank you.' She blinked, unexpected tears filling her eyes at the raw want in his voice. 'You don't look too bad yourself.'

They stood, caught in time just staring at each other, the pressure in the room intensifying until it was just the two of them, caught in a spotlight. Flora cleared her throat. 'Shall we go?' She didn't want to prolong the moment. Not tonight. Not when tomorrow meant moments such as this would be finished for ever.

Flora waited for him to open the door but he just stood there. 'I…er…I got you this. I know Christmas isn't for another couple of days but, well…' He held out a black velvet jewellery box.

Flora froze. He had never bought her jewellery before. Alex was usually a generous and perceptive gift buyer but jewellery buying was too intimate, a line he had never crossed before. Still, they were crossing all sorts of lines this week. Why not this one?

'For me?' She was aware how stupid the words were as she uttered them and he nodded, a faint smile playing on his lips as he did so.

'For you. Don't you want to open it?'

She reached out cautiously. 'I'm not sure,' she confessed. 'There's not a trick snake in there, is there?'

'One time, Flora, one time. And I was ten!'

'Okay, then.' The box was solid, heavier than she expected and she turned it around in her hands, the velvet soft against her skin. It wasn't new, she knew that at once; the hinges were tarnished and the velvet rubbed in places. She smiled over at Alex, her heart lifting with the discovery; she wasn't much of one for new, she preferred her possessions to have a history, a story.

She found the clasp and sprung it before carefully opening the lid and let out a little anticipatory breath she hadn't even been aware that she was holding. A necklace sparkled on the yellowing white satin cushion. Flora stole a quick look up at Alex. His face was impassive, as if he were waiting for her to comment on the weather or ask the time, but the strained set of his shoulders showed that he was waiting for her reaction. Slowly she hooked the necklace onto one newly manicured finger and drew it out of the box.

It was a two-tiered circlet of large, crystal beads designed to fall just below the neck, nestling on the collarbone. 'It's…' She shook her head, searching for the right words. 'It's perfect. How?' She couldn't complete the question.

'I knew where you bought the dress from so I popped in and said I wanted something to go with it. They remembered you quite clearly.' He took the necklace from her unresisting hand and moved behind her. She felt the cool heaviness of the beads settle around her neck, his fingers brush against the nape of her neck as he swept her hair aside, his breath on her skin as he leaned forward and clasped the necklace.

'It's nineteen fifties, like your dress, and made of the local Austrian crystal.' He let her hair fall back and stepped away. She instantly felt colder.

'It's absolutely gorgeous.' Flora put her hand up to her neck and fingered the chunky beads. 'Thank you, Alex. It's very thoughtful of you.' She turned around and rose on her tiptoes, pressing a kiss onto his cheek, inhaling his freshly washed scent as she did so. It *was* thoughtful—and it finished her dress off perfectly—but part of her wished that he hadn't bought it. That he'd stuck to books, or tickets or any of the usual gifts. Because each time she saw it she would be reminded of this night, of this trip. Each time she saw it she would be reminded of him. Not of Alex Fitzgerald, best mate and partner in crime, but of *this* Alex. The one who made her stomach turn over, her legs tremble and who made all good sense go flying out of the window.

The one she would say goodbye to in the morning. She put a hand up to her necklace and touched the central bead, the truth hitting her with brutal force. It wasn't going to be easy because she didn't want it to end. She wanted him to look at her with that mingling of desire and need and appreciation and humour for ever. But she'd made him a promise and she was going to keep it. No fuss, no repercussions, nothing was going to change. But, oh, how she wished it would.

'Come on.' She stepped back and turned to the door, her voice as artificially bright as her lipstick. 'We don't want to be late. Camilla has invited some local dignitaries and that means that you, my friend architect, have some schmoozing to do.'

'Oh, my goodness.' Flora stopped dead at the entrance to the dining room and stared, openmouthed, at the décor within. 'This is...'

'Like the ghost of Christmas kitsch just threw up in here?' Alex murmured in her ear.

'No!' She gave him a little shove. 'Well, only a little. It's very pretty though.'

Lights hung in the windows encircling the rooftop room; lit, dazzling, heavily bedecked Christmas trees stood to attention between each window like an army of greenery guarding the room. More lights were draped from a centre point in the ceiling, creating a marquee-like effect.

The lighting was all blues and whites, giving the illusion that they were standing in a particularly gaudy ice cave. The same colours were repeated on the tree decorations, on the tables that were dotted around the room, on the huge snowflakes and baubles that hung from the ceiling. A small band in the corner played a waltz, the music soaring over the glamorous guests as they stood chatting in small groups throughout the room.

'I hope the colour scheme isn't reflected in the drinks,' Flora whispered. 'I haven't drunk blue curaçao since university but I don't think it agrees with me.'

'It could be white drinks. What about advocaat?'

She shuddered. 'Now you're being mean. I thought we'd promised never to mention that New Year ever again.'

Luckily, before too many more embarrassing memories could be dredged up, a waitress stopped before them with a tray of kir royales, topped with raspberries. Flora took the glass Alex handed to her, thankful it was nothing more dangerous. 'Happy Christmas,' she said and raised her glass to him.

'Happy Christmas, Flora.' He toasted her back but the expression in his eyes was completely unreadable; his face wore the shuttered look she hated. It made him seem so far away. They only had tonight; she couldn't say goodbye early. She wasn't ready…

'Dance with me?'

He looked up at that, surprised. 'What? No one's dancing. It's still early.'

JESSICA GILMORE

JESSICA GILMORE# JESSICA GILMORE# JESSICA GILMORE# JESSICA GILMORE 219# JESSICA GILMORE 219

'So? If I can ski a red run on my second day you can be the first person onto the dance floor.'

'First couple,' he corrected her. 'There is no way on earth I would face that alone.' But he didn't demur any longer, holding his hand out to her and leading her to the centre of the room. There was a sudden hush as the other guests saw them step out but it was brief; the chatter starting up again as quickly as it had stopped.

Alex pulled her closer, one arm settling around her waist, the other clasping her hand. 'If we must do an exhibition dance then I am, for the first time, thankful that Minerva insisted that the whole wedding party needed to learn to dance properly.' It was a few years since the mandatory dance lessons but as he adjusted to the beat of the music it all began to come back. He could hear the teacher marking out the time as he had attempted to steer a mutinous Flora around the floor.

It was all so different now. She was pliant in his arms, letting him lead, her feet following his, her body at one with his—even if she did keep looking down at their feet.

'I don't remember you saying thank goodness at the time,' she pointed out, pausing to count under her breath. '*One* two three, *one* two three. It's a good job Minerva didn't want us all to salsa though.' She raised her eyes to his. They were luminous in the low light. 'Can you imagine how we'd look trying to salsa to this? We'd have to just do that slightly awkward shuffle instead.'

He tightened his arm, enjoying the feel of her so close to him, knowing that she was completely compliant, allowing him to take control. 'Did you know that the waltz was once considered scandalous?'

'Was it? Why?'

He lowered his voice. 'Just two people, a man, a woman, moving so closely together there's barely any space between them. His arm holding her to him, her hand clasped in his. He can feel her breasts pressing against his chest, smell the shampoo in her hair. If he wanted to…' He paused and looked directly into her upturned face, her mouth parted. 'If he wanted to kiss her then all he has to do is bend his head.'

'What if she didn't want him to kiss her?'

'Doesn't she?'

'Well…' Her lips curved into an enticing smile. 'Not in the middle of the dance floor. That really would cause a scandal. He would have to marry her if that happened.'

Alex blinked and she squeezed his hand reassuringly. 'In olden times I mean, silly. Don't worry, that wasn't a proposal.'

'Of course not.' But the words echoed round and round in his head. *Then he would have to marry her.*

The evening passed by in a quick blur as if someone had pressed fast forward. Alex lost Flora soon after their dance. Camilla whisked him away to meet, greet and act merry with the local dignitaries and influential industry movers and shakers while Flora was absorbed into a laughing group of revellers. The band switched to covers of popular songs and the dance floor was full.

But he could always find Flora; she stood out. Not just because of her height and her vibrant dress, but because she glowed as she moved across the floor.

He envied her even though he knew she deserved a carefree evening. He, on the other hand, was on his best behaviour, projecting the right image as he chatted to the VIPs Camilla needed him to impress.

Tomorrow it would all be over. This dazzling throng would pack away their finery ready for their trips home. He would return to Kent with Flora ready to resume their old friendship. Would it be enhanced by this week or tarnished? Maybe now they had given way to that old thrill of attraction they could move on—properly. She deserved a good man, someone to worship her, love her properly.

Alex folded his hands into tight fists, jealousy burning through him at the thought. How would he be able to stand there and smile as she held hands with another man, laughed up at another man, kissed another man?

There was only one way to bear it—to start thinking of his own future. A future beyond work and the need for success and recognition that had driven him so far, so fast. Was it so unthinkable that he too could have a long-term relationship? Maybe even marriage? Plenty of people had satisfactory, even successful lives together based on mutual respect and shared goals rather than passion and romance. Why not him?

He took another glass of kir royale from a passing waitress, mechanically nodding and smiling as the conversation around him turned to families and Christmas. His least favourite subject.

It wasn't that he didn't love spending the festive season with the Buckinghams. It wasn't as if they ever treated him as anything but one of the family. They didn't. He had been expected to muck in with the rest of them long before he'd started living there, peeling potatoes, setting the table, chopping logs for the fire—whatever was needed. Yes, they treated him like one of the family. But he *wasn't* family.

His own family had cast him out and one day the Buckinghams would too. Not on purpose but time wouldn't freeze. They wouldn't all return to the small Kentish village for the festive season for ever. One day Minerva would want to host Christmas, or Horry, if he ever looked up from his scalpel long enough to have a relationship. Or Flora would. Would there be a place for him in the family then? In ten years? In twenty?

He downed his drink. The solution was simple. It was time he thought about creating his own place. His own traditions and memories. Somewhere he built so he couldn't be cast out. The problem was he couldn't imagine anyone beside him but Flora.

And she deserved more…

He took another glass from a passing tray. And he watched her, trying to ignore the unwanted leap his heart gave when she smiled over at him. A secret smile of complicity.

Yes, she deserved more. But would she get it?

The thing was, he decided as he finished one glass and swapped it for another, that good things didn't always come to those who waited. After all, Flora hadn't had much luck with her past boyfriends. Just because he was prepared to do the right thing and stand aside didn't mean she would end up with someone who deserved her. It was all such a lottery. *He* could offer stability, space, affection. These were all good commodities in the trading place that was marriage. In return he would get a home. A place that was his.

It was a good trade.

Marriage.

Was he seriously thinking about it?

The room had darkened, the music quietening back to the classical waltzes so typical of Austria and the dance floor was now occupied by couples, the English swaying together awkwardly, the Austrians waltzing with the same grace he had admired on the ice rink and on the slopes.

Flora stood on the opposite side of the room, leaning against a chair and watching the dances, yearning on her face. Alex put his glass down and weaved his way over to her. He had drunk more than he usually allowed himself to; everything felt fuzzier, softer. Sweeter.

'Hi, have you been released early?'

'Time off for good behaviour. Having fun?'

'You know what…' she blinked at him, owlish in her solemn surprise '…I have. There are some really lovely people here.'

'Dance with me.' It wasn't a request and she obediently took his proffered hand, allowing him to lead her back onto the floor. She sank in close, her hand splayed on his back, and he could feel where every part of her touched him as if they weren't separated by layers of material but as if they were back in the ski lodge, learning each other anew.

Her head was on his shoulder, nestled in trustingly. They had trust. They had friendship.

They had passion.

It was a lot.

Alex stopped. 'Flora?'

'Mmm…why aren't we dancing?' She looked up at him, her mouth curved invitingly, and that was all he needed. Alex dipped his head and kissed her, a sweet, gentle caress.

She smiled up at him. 'That was nice. What was that for?'

'I wanted to.' He began to move again, slowing the steps down so that they were out of time with the music, dancing to their own private beat, their lips finding each other again, a deeper, intoxicating kiss. He was dimly aware that they were still moving, that the violins were soaring, the lights were low, but none of it was real. Only they were real. Just the taste of her, the feel of her, the scent of her. He wanted to sink deeper and deeper, to be absorbed by her, into her.

Only she was real. She made him real.

'Not here.' Flora's breath was ragged as she broke away. 'Not like that.'

He stared at her uncomprehendingly, still lost in the memory of her warmth.

'I mean…' She squeezed his hand, running her thumb over his palm, trailing fire with her touch. Fire that threatened to consume him. 'We're in the middle of a dance floor. I think we should take this back to our room.'

Of course. How could he have forgotten? How could he have been so swept up in the moment that he had lost track of where they were, forgotten that they weren't alone?

He swallowed. 'I warned you that the waltz was a scandalous dance.'

'You did,' she agreed. 'Am I quite compromised?'

"I think so…' His earlier thoughts came back to haunt him. Peace, stability, a family of his own… 'Unless we marry. What about it, Flora? Will you marry me?'

CHAPTER TEN

THE WALK BACK to the room seemed to take for ever. Every few steps they bumped into a group of Flora's new friends wanting to drag her off to the bar, to after parties, for midnight walks out in the snow.

She turned each of them down with a laughing non-committal reply but the whole situation didn't seem real. Her voice was too bright, her smile too wild and there was a buzzing in her ears as if she were in a waking dream.

Alex didn't say anything at all. His hand clasped hers tight; his eyes burned with that same strange intensity she had seen on the dance floor.

And his words echoed round and round in her head. *Will you marry me?*

Of course he had been joking. Of course. There was no doubt. Just because his fingers were gripping hers tightly, just because she had daydreamed a similar scenario more times than she had imagined winning the lottery didn't make it real.

Only…he had sounded serious.

What if he was serious?

No. Of course he wasn't because dreams didn't simply just come true. A dance floor, a waltz, beautiful lighting, champagne; that was the stuff of fairy tales, not real life. Not Flora's life.

But he *looked* serious.

She had been so desperate to get him back to the room but as they approached the door an unexpected caution hit her. Whatever was done and said when they got inside couldn't be unsaid, couldn't be undone. And his face was so very set. The passion and laughter wiped clear as if they had never been.

Flora took a deep breath as they walked into the room. It was her imagination, that was all, working on his words and twisting them into something more serious than intended. She needed to lighten up, enjoy these last few hours before it all changed back and she was back in her rags clutching a pumpkin.

Okay. Lightening up. 'Alone at last.' She smiled provocatively at him but there was no answering smile on his face.

'I meant it, you know. Marry me.'

Flora reached up to unclasp her necklace but at his quiet words her hands dropped helplessly to her side. 'No bended knee, no flash mob, no ring in my ice cream?' She tried to tease but the joke was flatter than one of her father's failed soufflés, and Alex didn't acknowledge it with as much as a flicker of an eyelid.

She walked over to the window and stared out. Ahead was darkness but if she looked up then the stars shone with an astonishing intensity, unfamiliar to a girl used to London's never fully darkened skies. Below Innsbruck was lit up like a toy town. Not quite real.

Like this moment.

'Why?'

She held her breath, hope fluttering wildly in

her chest. Would he say it? *Because I love you. I have always loved you.*

He didn't answer, not straight away. She heard him pace back and forth, imagined him shrugging off the tuxedo jacket, undoing his bow tie, running his hands through his disordered curls.

'Does it matter why?' he asked at last.

She still couldn't turn to face him but at his words hope's flutters became feebler and nausea began to swirl in her stomach.

'I think so, yes.' *Tell me, tell me,* she silently begged him. *Tell me what I need to hear and I'll believe you.*

Even though she knew it wouldn't be true.

'No one knows me like you do. You know everything, all the darkness, and you're still here.'

'Of course I am.'

'We know we're compatible. I think we could lead very comfortable, happy lives together. The sex is good—more than good. And marriage would tick other boxes too.'

Flora swallowed. Hope finally gave up and withered away. Her stomach still twisted with nausea but most thought and feeling drained away to a much-needed numbness. 'Great,' she murmured. Marriage as a box-ticking exercise. Just what she had always dreamed of. Maybe they could make a list and follow it up with a presentation on the computer.

'It would make things a lot easier for you as you change focus. I know money has been tight. That wouldn't be an issue any longer, and there's plenty of space at my house for a studio and storage.'

'Money, storage…' she repeated as if in a dream, the practical words not quite sinking in. 'And what about you? What's in it for you, apart from good sex?'

He didn't seem to hear the bitterness in her last words, just continuing as if this were a completely sane conversation. 'For me? No more dating, trying to be someone I'm not. Freedom to work—you wouldn't mind when work took me abroad, wouldn't expect me to check in every five minutes. There wouldn't be any misunderstandings, any expectations—you wouldn't want more than I can give.'

'No, I suppose I wouldn't.' Not now anyway. It wasn't as if he hadn't warned her, was it? She had chosen not to listen. Not to guard herself against this.

She wasn't numb now, she was cold. A biting chill working its way up from her toes, bone deep.

He hadn't noticed, was still listing soulless benefits as if it were next week's shopping list. 'And there would be no real adjustment. We know each other's bad habits, moods, and I get on with your family. Think about it, Flora. It makes perfect sense.'

'Yes, I can see that.' She turned at last. He had discarded his jacket and his tie, his shirt half un-tucked and unbuttoned, his hair falling over his forehead. He looked slightly dangerous, a little degenerate like the sort of regency rake who would kiss a girl on a dance floor and not care about the consequences.

And yet here he was offering a marriage of

convenience. If she said no—*when* she said no—then everything really would change. They might be able to sweep a week of passion under the carpet. They wouldn't be able to sweep this away.

Especially when every traitorous fibre of her wanted to say yes.

'I can't...' she said before she allowed herself to weaken.

His eyes blazed for one heartbreaking moment and then the shutters came down. 'Right. I see. Fine. Silly of me to think you would. Let's not mention it again.'

'I need more from marriage.' The words were tumbling out. 'I want love.'

A muscle worked in his cheek. 'I do love you, you know that. As much as I can.'

'But are you *in* love with me?'

She couldn't believe she'd asked that. The last taboo, more powerful than the kisses they had shared, the whispered intimacies. This, *this* was the big one. But she had to know. She took a deep, shuddering breath and waited. Would he?

Did he? All he had to do was tell her he loved her and she would be in.

He ran a hand through his hair. 'Do I care about you? Yes. Desire you? Absolutely. Like your company? You know I do. Isn't that enough?'

Flora shook her head. 'I wish it was,' she whispered. 'But I want more. I want the whole crazy, passionate, all-consuming love. I want to be the centre of someone's world and for my world to revolve around them.'

But he was shaking his head, a denial of her words, of her hopes and dreams. 'That's not real love, Flora. That's a crush at best, obsession at worst,' and with those calm words Flora felt something inside her crack clean in two.

'Oxytocin, serotonin. Hormones telling you lies. Love? It's unstable, it can't be trusted. But you're right. Marriage between us is a bad idea.' He stepped back and picked up his jacket, shrugging himself into it. 'I'm sorry I embarrassed you. If you'll excuse me, then I am going to get a drink. I'll see you later. Don't wait up.'

* * *

The plane was buzzing with festive spirit. Bags stuffed into the overhead lockers filled with brightly wrapped presents, people chatting eagerly to their seatmates—even strangers—about their plans for the next few days. Even the pilot made some flying reindeer jokes as he prepared them for take-off.

But the buzz didn't reach their two seats. They were ensconced in roomy first-class comfort. There were free drinks, legroom, food—but Alex and Flora sat stiffly as if they were crammed into the most cramped economy seat.

Flora was sleeping—or, Alex suspected, she was pretending to—and he was looking through documents as if the fate of Christmas depended on his memorising them by heart. If that had been the case then Christmas was in trouble; no matter how often he skimmed a sentence his brain could not make head or tail of it, his brain revolving round and round and round.

She'd said no. Even the person who knew him

best, who he thought loved him best, didn't want to risk her happiness on him.

And now he'd done exactly what he had sworn he would never do. He'd broken Flora's heart, tainted their friendship, ruined his relationship with her family. Because how could he possibly turn up there tomorrow ready to bask in Christmas cheer when he couldn't even look at Flora?

Especially as she couldn't look at him either. Oh, she was trying. She made stilted conversation, her smile too bright, her voice too cheery, but her eyes slid away when they reached his face, her body leaning away from his whenever they were close. Luckily his monosyllabic replies hadn't seemed too out of character when other people were around—most of the departing guests were similarly afflicted, suffering the effects of overindulgence the night before.

It wasn't a hangover that affected him, although heaven only knew he'd tried his best. Sitting in the bar until three a.m., drinking alone at the end, trying to block out the voices from his head.

You taint everything.

I can't marry you.

I want love.

What could he answer to that when he didn't even know what love was? The twisted obsession his father had had for his mother, so jealous he didn't even want to share her affection with their child? The grateful desperation he had shown towards his stepmother for deigning to notice him and the dark turning that had taken?

He didn't want or need that selfish emotion. There was a time when that made him feel invincible, as if he had an invisible armour protecting him from the follies that befell so many of his friends.

Now he just felt lost. Stuck in a labyrinth he didn't have the key for—only there was no princess holding a ball of string ready to guide him out. And there was no monster. *He* was the monster.

How could he return to Kent with her now? It was her home, not his. The only place he belonged to was the house he had designed in

Primrose Hill. But he didn't want to return there alone, to spend Christmas alone in a house without a heart.

Maybe it wasn't too late to grab a last-minute flight and head out again. He looked around the plane at the bland décor, the packed seats filled with strangers, the almost soothing signs telling him to sit back, switch his phone off, keep his seat belt on. He could spend Christmas Day on a flight. It almost didn't matter where to.

'Do you have to pick up presents and things before you head back home?' His throat scratched as he forced the words out, as if unaccustomed to speaking.

Flora's eyes opened a fraction. 'Yes, if that's okay.'

'I've ordered you a car. It'll run you back to yours and wait for you, as long as you need, then take you home to Kent.'

She sat up at that, any pretence at sleep forgotten. 'You're not coming back with me?'

'Not tonight, I have too much to do.'

'Too much to do on Christmas Eve? Everything's shut for the next few days. What on earth can't wait? But you are driving down tomorrow?'

He couldn't answer.

Her eyes flashed. 'We promised, Alex, we promised that we wouldn't let things change.'

Had she really believed they wouldn't? Had he? He closed his eyes, exhausted. 'We lied.'

There was no more to be said. Not for the last hour of the flight, not during the tedious business of disembarking, immigration and baggage collecting. Not as he saw the sign with his name on it and steered a mute Flora towards it.

'Can you drop my bags and skis off at my house on your way out?' he asked. 'You have your key?'

She turned to look at him, her face paler than usual, the white accented by the deep shadows under her eyes. 'You're not even travelling with me? How are you getting home?'

He shrugged. 'Train, Tube. My own two feet.'

'You're getting on the train? On Christmas Eve? It'll be packed!'

He couldn't explain it, the need to wander, to be anonymous in a vast sea of people where nobody knew him, judged him. 'I'll be fine. I just need some space.'

She stared at him sceptically and then turned away, the dismissive movement conveying everything. Hurting far more than he had expected. 'Suit yourself. You always do.'

He stood and watched her walk away. 'Merry Christmas, Flora.' But she was too far away and his words fell unheard.

The train was as unpleasant as Flora had forecast. Alex was unable to get a seat and so he stood for the fifteen-minute journey back into London, barricaded into his spot by other people's suitcases and bulging bags of presents. The carriage stank of sweat, alcohol, fried chicken and desperation, the air punctuated by a baby's increasingly desperate cries and the sounds of several computer games turned up to a decidedly antisocial volume.

No wonder he rarely travelled by public transport. Alex gritted his teeth and hung on; he deserved no better.

Not that anyone else seemed to be suffering. His fellow travellers seemed to be as full of Christmas Eve cheer as those on the plane, upbeat despite the conditions. But once he had finally got off the train and stood under the iconic glass curved roof of Paddington Station the last thing he wanted was to disappear underground and repeat the experience on a Tube train full of last-minute desperate shoppers, Christmas revellers and people freed from work and ready to celebrate. It was a couple of miles' walk to Primrose Hill but half of that was through Regent's Park and he could do with clearing his head.

Besides, he didn't want to risk bumping into Flora when she dropped his bags off. For the first time in his life he had no idea what to say to her.

It was hard not to contrast the grey, unseasonably warm day with the crisp air and snowy scenes he had left behind. Hard not to dwell on the fact that for the first time in a week he was alone.

Hard to face the reality that this was his future. He'd always thought of himself as so self-sufficient. Hardened.

He'd been lying to himself.

Alex bought a coffee from one of the kiosks, curtly refusing any festive flavourings, and set off, the last week replaying through his head on repeat, slowing down to dwell in agonising detail at every misstep. He shouldn't have kissed her. He shouldn't have allowed her to kiss him.

He shouldn't have proposed.

It shouldn't hurt so much that she said no…

He wandered aimlessly, not caring much where his feet took him. The back streets were an eclectic mix of tree-lined Georgian squares, post-war blocks and newer, shabbier-looking business premises. Like all of central London, the very wealthy rubbed shoulders with the poor; wine bars, delis and exclusive boutiques on one street, a twenty-four-hour supermarket and take-away on the next.

It wasn't until he hit Russell Square that Alex realised just how far he had walked—and how far out of his way he was. He stood for a moment in the middle of the old Bloomsbury square wondering what to do. Head into a pub and drink himself into oblivion? Keep walking until he was so exhausted the pain in his legs outweighed the weight in his chest? Just sit here in the busy square and gradually decompose?

Or run home, grab the car and head off to Kent. He'd be welcomed; he knew that. Flora would try her best to pretend everything was okay. But he didn't belong there, not really. He didn't belong anywhere or with anyone.

So what would it be? Pub, walk or wither away in the middle of Bloomsbury? He leaned against a bench, unsure for the first time in a really long time which way he should go, looking around at the leafless trees and railings for inspiration when a brown sign caught his eye. Of course! The British Museum was just around the corner. He could while away the rest of the afternoon in there. Hide amongst the mummies and the ancient sculptures and pretend that it wasn't Christmas Eve. Pretend he had somewhere to go, someone to care.

Pretend he was worth something.

His decision was made; only as he rounded the corner and hurried towards the huge gates shielding the classically inspired façade of the famous museum he was greeted, not by open gates and doors and a safe neutral place, but by iron bars and locks. The museum was closed.

Alex let out a deep breath, one he hadn't even known he was holding, gripping the wrought-iron bars as if he could push them apart. No sanctuary for him. Maybe it was a judgement. He wasn't worthy, no rest for him.

He stared at the steps, the carved pillars, the very shut doors. It was strange he hadn't visited the museum in the eleven years he'd lived in London; after all, it was visiting this very building that had first triggered his interest in building design. The neoclassical façade built to house the ancient treasures within. He used to come here every summer with his grandmother.

With his grandmother...

When had that stopped? When had he stopped seeing her? Before he was ten, he was pretty sure. She took him out a couple of times his first year at prep school, had visited regularly before then, although he had never been allowed an overnight stay. And then? Nothing.

No cards, no Christmas presents. Nothing. He hadn't even thought to ask where she had gone—after all, his father had made it very clear that it was Alex who was the problem. Alex who was innately unlovable.

But it wasn't normal, was it? For a grandparent to disappear so completely from a child's life? If she had blamed Alex for her daughter's death then she wouldn't have been around at all. And surely even his father would have told him if she had died.

There was something missing, something rotten at the heart of him and he had to know what it was, had to fix it. Fix his friendship with Flora.

Be worthy of her...

He couldn't ask his mother why she couldn't

love him, why she'd left him. He couldn't expect any meaningful dialogue with his father. But maybe his grandmother had some answers. If he could find her.

He had to find her. He couldn't go on like this.

Christmas Eve was usually Flora's favourite day of the year. All the anticipation, the air of secrecy and suppressed excitement. The rituals, unchanging and sacred. They were usually all home and unpacked by late afternoon before gathering together in the large sitting room to admire the tree and watch Christmas films. The last couple of years they had pretended that the films were to amuse the children—but the children usually got bored and wandered off leaving the adults rapt, enthralled by stories they had watched a hundred times before.

Then a takeaway to spare Flora's dad cooking for this one evening, before stockings were hung. Milk and carrots would be put out for the reindeers, home-made gingerbread and a snifter of brandy for Father Christmas himself and then the children were bundled off to bed. The last few years Minerva and Flora's mother had stayed behind to babysit the children and put the last few touches to presents but the rest of the family would disappear off to the pub for a couple of hours, finishing off at Midnight Mass in the ancient village church.

She loved every unchanging moment of it.

But this year it would all be different.

What if she had said yes? Right now she and Alex could be walking into the house hand in hand to congratulations, tears, champagne.

But it would all have been a lie.

Flora took a deep breath, trying to steady her nerves as the car Alex had ordered for her rolled smoothly through the village towards the cottage her parents had bought over thirty years before, but her hands were trembling and her stomach tumbling with nervous anticipation. They must never know. Alex thought they would blame him but she knew better; they would blame her for driving him away.

She needed some air, time to compose herself before the onslaught of her family. 'This will be fine, thanks,' she said to the driver as they reached the bottom of her lane. 'I can walk from here.'

Flora stood for a moment gulping in air before shrugging her weekend bag onto her back and picking up the shopping bags full of presents. The bags were heavy and her back was aching before she had got more than halfway down the lane but she welcomed the discomfort. It was her penance.

The cottage stood alone at the end of the lane, a low-roofed half-timber, half-redbrick house surrounded by a wild-looking garden and fruit trees. Her father grew most of his own vegetables and herbs and kept noisy chickens in the back, although he was too soft-hearted to do more than collect their eggs.

The house was lit up against the grey of a late December afternoon, smoke wafting from the chimney a welcome harbinger. All she wanted to do was curl up in front of the fire and mourn but instead Flora pinned a determined smile onto her face and pushed open the heavy oak front door.

Game face on. 'Merry Christmas,' she called as the door swung open.

'Flora!' 'Aunty Flora!' 'Darling.' She was almost instantly enveloped in hugs and kisses, her coat removed, bags taken from her aching arms, drawn into the sitting room, a mince pie put into one hand, a cup of tea into the other as the chatter continued.

'How was Austria? Did you see snow?'

'Your scarf looked lovely in that picture. Congratulations, darling.'

'We need to talk strategy.' Minerva, of course. 'Boxing Day you are mine. No running off.'

'Nice journey back, darling?'

And the inevitable: 'Where's Alex?' 'Didn't Alex travel with you?' 'Did you leave Alex in Austria?'

If she had come back to a quiet house. If it had just been Flora and her dad, she sitting at the wide kitchen counter while he bustled and tasted and stirred. Then she might have cracked.

But the tree was in the corner of the room, decorated to within an inch of its life and blazing with light, her nieces were already at fever-pitch point and for once nobody was asking when she was going to get a real job/move out of that poky room/get a boyfriend/grow up.

So she smiled and agreed that yes, the scarf looked lovely; yes, Minerva could have all the time she needed; yes, there was plenty of snow and guess what, she'd even been on a horse-drawn sleigh. And no, Alex wasn't with her, he had been delayed but he should be with them tomorrow.

And if she crossed her fingers at that last statement it wasn't because she was lying. It was because she was hoping. Because now she was here she couldn't imagine Christmas without him. She couldn't imagine a life that didn't have him in it.

And even though she wished that he loved her the way that she loved him. And even though she would have given everything for his proposal to have come from his heart and not his head, she still wished he were here. Even if it was as friends. Because friends was still something special. Something to cherish.

She needed to tell him. Before he sealed himself away. Before he talked himself into utter isolation.

'I'm just going to take my bags upstairs. No, it's okay, thanks, Greg,' she assured her brother-in-law. 'I can manage. Besides...' she looked mock sternly at her giggling nieces '...I don't want any peeping.' She kissed her still-chattering mother on the cheek and went back into the hallway to retrieve her bags and hoist them up the wide carpeted staircase that led to the first floor and then up the winding, painted wooden stairs to the attic. There were just two bedrooms up here, sharing a small shower room. To the left was Flora's room, to the right a small box room they had converted into a room for Alex.

His bedroom door was ajar and Flora couldn't help peeking in as she turned. The bed had been made up with fresh linen and towels were piled onto the wicker chair in the corner. An old trunk

lay at the foot of the bed—his old school trunk—
a blanket laid across the top. A small bookshelf
held some books but otherwise it was bare. Spar-
tan. He had never allowed himself to be too at
home here. Or anywhere. No wonder he was
such an expert packer.

Flora's room was a stark contrast. It was more
than twice the size of his with a wide dormer
window as well as a skylight. Old toys, books
and ornaments were still displayed on the shelves
and on the white, scalloped dressing table and
chest of drawers she had thought so sophis-
ticated when she was twelve. Old posters of
ponies and boy bands were stuck to her walls
and a clutter of old scarves, old make-up and
magazines gave the room a lived-in air.

She dropped her bags thankfully in a corner
of the room and pulled her phone out of her
pocket. The message light flashed and Flora's
heart lurched with hope as she eagerly scanned
it, but, although she had received at least a million emails urging her to buy her last-minute
Christmas gifts Right Now, been promised the

best rate to pay off her Christmas debts by several credit-card companies and a very good deal on sexual enhancement products, there was nothing at all from Alex.

Swallowing back her disappointment, she stared thoughtfully at her screen. Call or text? Texting would be easier, give her a chance to phrase her words carefully. But maybe this shouldn't be careful. It had to be from the heart. She pressed his number before she could talk herself out of it and listened to the dial tone, her heart hammering.

She was so keyed up it didn't register at first that the voice at the other end wasn't Alex but his voicemail message. 'Darn it,' she muttered while his slightly constrained voice informed her that he wasn't available right now but would get back to her as soon as he could.

'Alex,' she said quickly as soon as it beeped. 'It's me. Come home. Please? It's not the same without you. We all miss you. We'll be okay, I promise. Just come home. Come home for Christmas.'

She clicked the hang-up icon and let the phone drop onto her bed. She had done all she could. It was up to him now.

CHAPTER ELEVEN

HOW HE REMEMBERED the address, Alex had no idea. He must have written it on enough letters that somehow he had retained the information, lying dormant until his need unlocked it once again. It took less than an hour of research to ascertain that his grandmother was still alive and living in the same house. But as he drove along the leafy, prosperous-looking road it was all completely unfamiliar and doubts began to creep in.

What if he had got the name and address wrong?

Or worse, what if he had got them right and she didn't want to see him?

He pulled up outside a well-maintained-looking white house and killed the engine. What was he doing? It was Christmas Eve and he was about to drop in, unannounced, on a long-lost relative who probably didn't want to see him. He must be crazy. Alex gripped the steering wheel and swore softly. But then he remembered Flora's face as she walked away from him at the airport. Disappointed, defeated. If there was any way he could put things right, he would.

And this might help.

The house looked shut up. Every curtain was drawn and there was no sign of light or life anywhere. The driveway was so thickly gravelled that he couldn't step quietly no matter how lightly he trod, and the crunch from each step echoed loudly, disturbing the eerie twilight silence. Any minute he expected a neighbour to accost him but there was no movement anywhere. It was like being in an alternative universe where he was the last soul standing.

The door was a substantial wooden oval with an imposing brass door knocker. It was cold and heavy as he lifted it, making far more of a bang than he expected when he rapped it on the door. He stood listening to the echo disturb the absolute silence, shivering a little in the murky air.

Alex shifted from foot to foot as he waited, straining to hear any movement in the house. He was just debating whether to try again or give up, half turning to walk away, when the door swung open.

'Oh, you're not the carol singers.' He turned back, words of explanation ready on his tongue when he found himself staring into a pair of familiar green-grey eyes, eyes growing round, hope and shock mingled in their depths. 'Alex? Is it really you?'

'You're not watching the films?' Flora's dad looked up from the pastry he was expertly rolling out and smiled at her. 'It's *The Muppet Christmas Carol.*'

'I know.' Flora wandered over to the oak and marble counter where her father practised his recipes and slipped a finger into the bowl of fragrant home-made mincemeat, sucking the sweet, spicy mixture appreciatively. 'Mmm, this is gorgeous. What's the secret ingredient?'

'Earl Grey and lemon.' He nodded at her finger. 'Dip that again and I'll chop it off. I thought the Muppets were your favourite?'

'They are.' Flora slid onto a high stool and leaned forward, propping her chin in her hands as she watched her father work. The pastry was a perfect smooth square as he began to cut out the rounds. 'Only I peeped in and Minerva, the twins and Greg are all curled up on the sofa. They looked so sweet I didn't want to disturb them.'

'They wouldn't have minded.'

'I know, but it's not often I see Minerva so relaxed. She might have wanted to start talking marketing strategy or buzz creation and then the film would have been ruined for everyone.'

'That's very thoughtful of you.' Her mother bustled into the kitchen, her phone in her hand. 'Great news, darling. Horry's colleague wants to work Christmas, bad break-up apparently, so she'd rather work. Awful for her but it means Horry can come home this evening after all. Now we just need Alex and the whole family is together again.'

Guilt punched Flora's chest and she resisted the urge to look at her phone to see if he'd responded. 'I'm sure he'll be here as soon as he can.'

'We're all very excited about your scarves.' Her mother filled the kettle and began to collect cups from the vast dresser that dominated the far wall. The kitchen used to be two rooms but they had been knocked into one and a glass-roofed extension added to make it a huge, airy, sun-filled space filled with gadgets, curios and the bits and bobs Flora's dad couldn't resist: painted bowls, salt and pepper pots, vintage jugs and a whole assortment of souvenirs. Saucepans hung from a rack on the ceiling, there were planted herbs on every window sill and the range cooker usually had something tasty baking, bubbling or roasting, filling the air with rich aromas.

'It doesn't seem quite real.' Flora grimaced. 'I'm sure Minerva will change that. She was hissing something about Gantt charts earlier.'

'She's right, you should take this seriously.' Her mother added three teaspoons of tea to the large pot and topped it with the boiled water. No teabags or shortcuts in the Buckingham kitchen. 'I don't know why it's taken you so long. It's obvious you should have been focusing on this, not wasting your talents on that awful pub chain. Those disgusting neon lemons…' She shuddered.

Flora stared at her mother. 'I thought you wanted me to have a steady job.' She couldn't keep the hurt out of her voice. 'You're always asking me when I'm going to settle down—in a job, a relationship, a place of my own.'

'No,' her mother contradicted as she passed Flora a cup of tea. Flora wrapped her hands around it, grateful for its warmth. 'I wanted you to have direction. To know where you *wanted* to go. You always seemed so lost, Flora. Vet school to compete with the twins, interior design to fit in with Alex. I just wanted you to follow your own heart.'

'It's not always that easy though, is it? I mean, sometimes your heart can lead you astray.' To Flora's horror she could feel tears bubbling up.

She swallowed hard, trying to hold back the threatening sob, ducking her head to hide her eyes. She should have known better. Nothing ever escaped Dr Jane Buckingham's sharp eyes.

'Flora?' Her mother's voice was gentle and that, combined with the gentle hug, pushed Flora over the edge she had been teetering on. It was almost a relief to let the tears flow, to let the sobs burst out, easing the painful pressure in her chest just a little. Her mother didn't probe or ask any more, she just held Flora as she cried, rubbing her back and smoothing her hair off her wet cheeks.

It was like being a child again. If only her mother could fix this. If only it *were* fixable.

It took several minutes before the sobs quietened, the tears stopped and the hiccups subsided. Flora had been guided to the old but very comfortable chintzy sofa by the window, her tea handed to her along with yet another of her father's mince pies. She curled up onto the cushions and stared out of the window at the pot-filled patio and the lawn beyond.

'I won't ask any awkward questions,' her mother promised as she sat next to her. 'But if you do want to talk we're always here. You do know that, I hope, darling.'

Flora nodded, not quite trusting herself to speak. She didn't often confide in her parents, not wanting to see the disappointed looks on their faces, not to feel that yet again she was a let-down compared to her high-flying siblings.

But she wasn't sure she could carry this alone. Not any more.

'Alex asked me to marry him.'

She didn't miss the exchange of glances between her parents. They didn't look shocked, more saddened.

'I wondered if it was Alex. You've always loved him so.'

She had no secrets, it seemed, and there was no point in denying it. She nodded. 'But he doesn't love me. He thought marriage would be sensible. He said I would have financial stability and storage for my designs.'

'Oh.'

'I mean, I didn't expect sonnets but I didn't think anyone would ever suggest storage as a reason for marriage.' Flora was aware she sounded bitter. 'How could I say yes? It would have been so wrong for both of us. Only now he's not here and I miss him so much...'

Her mother patted her knee. 'Have I ever told you how your father and I met?'

Flora stifled a sigh. Here it came, the patented Dr Jane Buckingham anecdote filled with advice. 'You were flatmates,' she muttered.

'For a year,' her father said, standing back to survey the trays of finished mince pies.

'And then you went out for dinner and looked into each other's eyes and the rest is history.' Perfect couple with their perfect jobs and a perfect home and nearly perfect children. The story had been rehashed in a hundred interviews.

'I think I fell in love with your mother the moment I saw her,' her father said, a reminiscent tone in his voice. 'But I didn't think I was good enough for her. I was a hobby baker and trainee food journalist and there she was, a junior doctor. Brilliant, fierce, dedicated. I didn't know what to say to her. So I didn't really say anything at all.'

Flora's mother picked up the tale. 'But when I came off shift—exhausted after sixty hours on my feet, malnourished after grabbing something from the hospital canteen—I would walk in and there would be something ready for me. No matter what time. A filo pie and roasted vegetables at two in the morning, piles of fluffy pancakes heaped with fruit at seven a.m. Freshly made bread and delicious salads at noon.' A soft smile curved her mother's lips. 'Do you remember when I said I missed falafel and you made them? They weren't readily available then,' she told her daughter. 'It was just a passing comment but I got home two days later to find freshly made falafel and home-made hummus in the fridge.'

'You old romantic.' Flora smiled over at her dad.

'I still barely spoke to her,' he admitted. 'I didn't know what to say. But I listened.'

'And then on Valentine's Day I came in, so tired I could barely drag myself in through the door, and waiting for me was the most beautiful breakfast. Home-made granola, eggs Benedict, little pastries. And I understood what he'd been telling me for the last year. Not with words but with food, with his actions. So I slept and then I took *him* out for dinner to say thank you. We got married six months later.'

'If you want to be wooed with flowers and lovely words, then Alex is never going to be the man for you, Flora,' her father added. 'And maybe he really does think storage and stability is enough. But *maybe* those words mask something more. You need to dig a little deeper. See what's really in his heart. A pancake isn't always just a pancake.'

Flora bit into the mince pie. The pastry was perfect, firm yet melting with a lemony tang, the filling spicy yet subtle. When it came to food her dad was always spot on. Maybe he was right here as well.

'Thank you,' she said, but she couldn't help

checking her phone as she did so. Nor could she deny the sharp stab of disappointment when she saw that Alex hadn't replied.

Was her father right? Was Alex's matter-of-fact proposal a cover for deeper feelings and if so would she be able to live with someone who would never be able to say what was in their heart? Live with the constant uncertainty? Flora sighed; maybe she was clutching at straws and there was no hidden meaning. Maybe storage was just that. The question was how willing was she to find out and what compromises was she willing to make?

And if a practical marriage was the only way to keep him, then could she settle for that when the alternative was losing him for ever?

'That's you and your mother. You must have been about eighteen months.'

Alex stared at the photo, lovingly mounted in a leather book. It was one of several charting his mother's brief life from a smiling baby to a wary-looking teen, a shy young bride to a proud mother.

'She looks…'

'Happy?' his grandmother supplied. 'She was, a lot of the time.'

Alex struggled to marry this side of his mother with the few pieces of information his father had begrudgingly fed him. He put the album back onto the low wooden coffee table and stared around the room in search of help.

Alex had never really known any of his grandparents but he had always imagined them in old, musty houses filled with cushions, lace tablecloths and hordes of silver-framed photos. The light, clean lines of his grandmother's sitting room were as far from the dark rooms of his dreams as the slim woman opposite with her trendy pixie cut and jeans and jacket was from the grey-haired granny of his imagination.

'My father said she cried all the time. That she hated being a mother, hated me. That's why…' he faltered. 'That's why she did what she did.'

His grandmother closed her eyes briefly. 'I

should have tried harder, Alex. I should have fought for you. Your father made things so difficult. I was allowed a day here, a day there, no overnight stays or holidays and I was too scared to push in case he locked me out completely—but he did that anyway. In the end my letters were returned, my gifts sent back. He said it was too hard for you to be reminded of the past, that he wanted you to settle with your stepmother.'

Letters, gifts? His father hadn't just returned material items. He had made sure that Alex would never have a loving relationship with his family.

His grandmother twisted her hands. 'If I had tried harder then I could have made sure you knew about your mother. The colours she liked, her favourite books, the way she sang when she was happy. But most importantly I could have told you that she loved you. Because she did, very, very much. But she wasn't well. She didn't think she was a good enough mother, she worried about every little thing—every cry was a reminder that she was letting you down. Every tiny incident a reminder that she was failing you. In the end she convinced herself that you would be better off without her.'

Alex blinked, heat burning his eyes. 'She was wrong.'

'I know. I should have made her get help.' She closed her eyes and for a moment she looked much older, frailer, her face lined with grief. 'But she was good at hiding her feelings and she was completely under your father's control. He couldn't admit that she wasn't well; it didn't fit with his vision of the perfect family. And so she got more adept at denying she was struggling but all the time she was sinking deeper and deeper. I knew something was wrong but every time I tried to talk to her she would back away. So I stopped trying, afraid that I would lose her. But I lost her anyway. And I lost you.' Her voice faltered, still raw with grief all these years later.

Alex swallowed. 'Can you tell me about her now?'

His grandmother blinked, her eyes shiny with

tears, and glanced up at the clock on the mantelpiece. 'Goodness, is that the time? My son—your uncle—will be collecting me soon. I always spend Christmas Eve at their house. You have three cousins, all younger than you, of course, but they will be so excited to meet you.'

Christmas Eve, how could he have forgotten? 'I'm sorry, I didn't think...'

His grandmother carried on as if he hadn't spoken. 'I'm just going to ask him to collect me in the morning instead. You will stay for dinner? There's a room if you want to spend the night. We have a lifetime of catching up to do. Unless, there must be somewhere you need to be. A handsome boy like you. A wife?' Her eyes flickered to his left hand. 'A girlfriend?'

Alex shook his head. 'No,' he said. 'There isn't anyone.' But as he spoke the words he knew they weren't entirely true.

Alex wasn't sure how long his grandmother was gone. He was lost in the past, going through each album again, committing each photo to heart. His mother as a young girl on the beach, her graduation photos, her wedding pictures. There was a proud, proprietorial gleam in his father's eyes that sent a shiver snaking down Alex's spine. Love wasn't meant to be selfish and destructive; he might not know much but he knew that. Surely it was supposed to be about support, putting the other person first. Shared goals.

Pretty much what he had offered Flora.

And yet it hadn't been enough…

His brooding thoughts were interrupted as his grandmother backed into the room holding a tray and Alex jumped to his feet to take it from her. 'Thank you,' she said. 'There's not much, I'm afraid. I'm at your uncle's until after New Year so rations are rather sparse.' She directed him to the round table near the patio doors and Alex placed the tray onto it, carefully setting out the bowls of piping-hot soup and the plates heaped with crackers, cheese and apples.

'It looks perfect. Thank you for rearranging your plans. You really didn't have to.'

'I wanted to. Everything's arranged and your

uncle has asked me to let you know that you
are welcome to come too tomorrow—or at any
point over the holidays. For an hour or a night o
the whole week. Whatever you need. There's nc
need to call ahead, please. If you want to come
just turn up, I'll make sure you have the address
Now sit down, do. I tend to eat in here—I don'
like eating in the kitchen and sitting in sole stat
in the dining room would be far too lonely.
rarely use it now.' She sighed. 'This house is fa
too big but it's so crammed with memories—
of my husband, of your mother—that I hate the
idea of leaving.'

'When did my grandfather die?' Another fam
ily member he would never know.

'When your mother was eighteen. It hit he
very hard. She was a real daddy's girl. I some
times think that's why she fell for your father
He was so certain of everything and she wa:
still so vulnerable. Your grandfather's death hac
ripped our family apart and we were all alone ir
our grief. I still miss him every day. He was my
best friend. He made every day an adventure.'

The soup was excellent, thick, spicy and warming, but Alex was hardly aware of it. Best friends? So it *could* work.

'That's the nicest epitaph I ever heard. He must have been an amazing man.'

How would Alex be remembered after he died? Hopefully as a talented and successful architect. But was that enough?

No. It wasn't. He wanted someone to have that same wistful look in their eye. That same mingled grief, nostalgia, affection and humour. No. He didn't want just *someone* to remember him that way.

He wanted Flora to. He wanted every day to be an adventure with his best friend. Not because it was safe and made sense. No. Because he loved her.

CHAPTER TWELVE

FLORA WOKE WITH a start, rolling over to check her phone automatically. Five a.m. and still no answer from Alex.

She rolled onto her back and stared at the luminous green stars still stuck to her ceiling. It had been a typical Christmas Eve; Horry had turned up during dinner, ready to hoover up all the leftover rice, pakoras and dahl, and then Greg had insisted on babysitting so that Minerva and Flora's mother could join the rest of their family for a couple of drinks before they all trooped to the ancient Norman church for the short and moving celebration of Midnight Mass. It wasn't often they were all together like this, but it just made Alex's absence all the more achingly obvious. Flora had tried not to spend the whole evening checking her phone. She had failed miserably, barely taking part in the conversation and mouthing her way through the carols.

Still no word. She just needed to know he was okay.

No, she was kidding herself. She wasn't that altruistic. She wanted to *know*, to look deeper, to see if somewhere, deep inside, he cared for her the way she so desperately wanted him to.

And if not to ask herself if that was all right. If all he was capable of offering was friendship mixed with passion, then should she agree to marry him anyway—because she would still be with him? Was it settling or being pragmatic? Selling herself short or grabbing the opportunity with both hands?

Although it was rather moot; having said no once, she wasn't sure how to let him know if she did change her mind. It wasn't exactly something you could drop into conversation.

Flora turned her pillow over, plumping it back up with a little more force than was strictly necessary, and attempted to snuggle back down; but it was no use. She was wide awake. Not the pleasurable anticipatory tingle of a Christmas morning but the creeping dread that nothing would ever be the same again.

Well, she could lie here and brood or she could get up, make coffee and make a plan. She reached for her phone again and the sudden light illuminated her room and the bags of presents still piled in the corner. It was an unwritten law that all presents had to be snuck under the Christmas tree without the knowledge of anyone else in the household. Flora and Alex usually spent most of the early hours trying to catch the other out—a heady few hours of ambush, traps and whispered giggles because it was also a sternly enforced law that nobody could get up before seven a.m., the edict a hangover from her childhood.

She swung her legs out of the bed, feeling for her slippers in the dark and shrugging on the old vintage velvet dressing gown Alex had bought her for her sixteenth birthday, before padding quietly across the room to retrieve the bags. The house was in darkness and, not wanting to wake anyone else up, she switched on the torch on her phone to help guide her down the windy stairs. Alex's door was still ajar, the empty room dark.

Her bags were bulky and it was all Flora could do to get them quietly along the landing and down the main stairs. Every rustle of paper, every muffled bang as the bag hit the bannister made her freeze in place, but finally she stepped over the creaky last step and into the hallway. Not for the first time she cursed her mother's decision to furnish the wide hall as a second sitting area. Not only did she have to dodge the hat stand, umbrella stand and the hall table, but she also had to weave around a bookcase and a couple of wing-backed chairs before she reached the safety of the sitting-room door.

Flora froze, her hand on the handle as she clocked the faint light seeping under the door? Another early riser? She could have sworn she had heard all her family make their stealthy present-laying trips soon after she had gone to bed, and it was far too quiet to be either of her nieces.

One of them had probably left the light on, that was all. She turned the handle and nudged the door open with her hip as she lugged the two bags into the room, turning to place them next to the tree…

Only to jump back when she saw a shadowy figure already kneeling under the tree. Grey with tiredness, hair rumpled and still in the clothes she had seen him in yesterday morning, on his knees as he added his own gifts to the pleasingly huge pile. 'Alex?'

He rocked back onto his heels. 'Merry Christmas, Flora.'

Her throat swelled and she swallowed hard, so many things to say and she had no idea which one to start with. 'You're here?' Great, start with the blindingly obvious. 'I tried calling…'

'I know. I got your message, thank you.'

'Where have you been?'

'That's a long story.' He nodded at the bags lying forgotten at her feet. 'Shall I pretend I haven't seen those and go and put some coffee on?'

She blinked, trying to clear her head, take

in that he was actually here, that he had come home. 'Yes. Coffee. Thanks.'

The corners of his mouth quirked up in a brief smile. 'Good. I could kill for one of your dad's mince pies as well.'

Normally Flora took her time placing her gifts, making sure they were spread out, tucked away, but right now she didn't care, chucking them onto the pile haphazardly with no care for the aesthetic effect. She switched off the lamps and sidled out of the room, closing the door quietly behind her before turning into the kitchen.

The scent of coffee was as welcome as the sight of Alex. Really here, reassuringly here, leaning against the counter, a mince pie in one hand, a mug in the other. 'Nothing says Christmas like your dad's baking.'

'That was the title of his last interview.' Flora leaned over and stole a crumb off his plate. 'It's good to see you, Alex.' It didn't feel like less than twenty-four hours since they had parted; it felt like a lifetime.

'I'm sorry I just took off but I needed some

time, some space. I took your advice. I looked up my mother's family.'

Whatever Flora had been expecting, it wasn't this. 'You did? I thought you didn't know where they were?'

'I didn't. Only since you mentioned them the idea was niggling away at the back of my mind. You were right, there had to be someone out there. And then I remembered, when I was a little boy I used to see my grandmother some-times—and I wrote to her a lot. I remembered enough of her address to be able to track her down.'

'What it is to have a photographic memory.'

'Turns out it comes in useful.'

'So.' Flora felt unaccountably shy. 'What was she like? Did you meet her?'

To her surprise Alex laughed. 'Nothing like I expected, very chic, rather cool and very lovely. You'll like her, Flora. And it was as if all the missing pieces just slotted together. She had an-swers and photos and she knew.'

'Knew what?'

His voice broke. 'That my mother loved me. She didn't kill herself because she hated me. She killed herself because she thought she was letting me down. It was her illness that was to blame, not me.'

Tears burned the backs of her eyes, her throat. How could he have lived all these years believing it was his fault? How could his father have allowed him to? All awkwardness, all restraint disappeared as Flora reached over to grab his hand, her fingers enfolding his. 'Of course it was—and of course she loved you. How could she not have?'

'She hung on for two years after I was born, terrified and so unhappy, but she tried. She really tried. If she'd got help it would all have been so different but she was in denial and my father thought that she was weak. He didn't want her talking to anyone but him.'

'If anyone's to blame he is. For all of it. For your mother, for taking your stepmother's side, for allowing you to leave home.'

'I think I know that now. The stupid thing is I

have spent my whole life wishing I had a family and a home and yet I had one all along.'

Flora looked down at the counter. 'With your grandmother.'

'No.' His voice softened. 'With you.'

She looked up, startled at his words. Her eyes locked onto his and her pulse began to thump at the look in his eyes. It was more than the desire she had enjoyed over the last week, more than the candid friendship of the last twenty years. It was new, unknown and so intense she could barely breathe. 'I'm glad you know that. No matter what happened with you and me your home is here...'

'I know that but that's not what I mean. I mean that wherever you are, Flora, that's where I belong. London, Kent, Bali, Austria. My house, your room or a tent in the pouring rain. I could lose everything tomorrow and as long as you were with me I wouldn't mind. You...' His voice cracked. 'You make every day an adventure, Flora, and I was too blind or too scared to see it before.'

The blood was rushing in her ears and she had to grip the counter tightly, afraid that she might fall without its solid support. 'Me?'

'I think I've always known it—from the very first day when you helped me make a den. Remember? I was running away but I wasn't scared because I'd found someone to be with. But I didn't want to face it. I didn't want to taint you. My father said I ruined everything and everyone I touched and, oh, Flora, I didn't want to ruin you.'

'You won't, you couldn't.'

'When I asked you to marry me I was a fool. I thought I meant those things, those sensible reasons, the list of positives, but really I was a coward. I was too afraid to tell you what I really meant. I wanted to tell you that you were the most beautiful woman in the ballroom, that I couldn't take my eyes off you all night, that you were my best friend and that I loved you and didn't want to spend a single second of my life away from you. That's what I should have said.'

Flora blinked hard, willing the tears not to fall. 'It's a little more convincing than storage.'

'If I'd told you all this then, would you have said yes?'

She nodded, unable to get the words out.

'And…' he stepped around the counter so that he was right next to her, turning her unresisting body so that she faced him, cupping her face in his hands and looking down at her, tenderness in his eyes '…if I ask you now?'

Flora smiled up at him, her voice scarcely more than a whisper. 'Why don't you ask me and see?'

Laughter flashed in his eyes as he took her hand in his. 'No flash mobs, no rings in ice cream, no sonnets. Just you and me, Flora. Just like it's always been.'

She nodded, her chest so swollen with happiness she thought she might drift away.

'Flora Prosperine Buckingham, would you do me the incredible honour of being my best friend, my companion, my lover, my confidante and my partner in adventure every day for the rest of my life?'

'I can't think of anyone I'd rather spend my life with.' Flora looked at him, at the ruddy, disordered curls, the freckles, the long-lashed eyes, and her heart turned over with love. 'Of course I'll marry you. I think I fell in love with you too, that day in the lane. You were so determined and so brave. I just wanted to make it all better.'

'You did, you do. It just took me far too long to notice.'

'Look.' She pointed upwards to the beam overhead. 'Mistletoe.'

'I don't need mistletoe to tell me to kiss you, not any more.' Alex leaned forward and brushed her mouth with his. 'Merry Christmas, Flora.'

'Merry Christmas, Alex.' She could finally say the words she had been holding in for so long. 'I love you.'

He looked over at the grandfather clock in the corner. 'We still have ninety minutes before the household's allowed to get up. Can you think of any way to spend it?'

Flora rose onto her tiptoes and allowed herself to kiss him properly, deeply, lovingly. Her fiancé, her man, her best friend. 'I'm sure we can think of something...'

* * * * *